DEVONSHIRE CREAM

A Mrs. Millet & Mrs. Hark Mystery

by

Margaret Searles

WIP

Wrinklers Press
McKinleyville, California

DEVONSHIRE CREAM

This book is a work of fiction. All characters and incidents mentioned herein are figments of the author's imagination. Any resemblance to actual events, locales or persons, living or dead, is entirely coincidental.

Queries regarding rights and permissions should be addressed to:
Wrinklers Press
P.O. Box 2745
McKinleyville, CA 95519-2745.

First paperback printing, 2005

Devonshire Cream / by Margaret Searles
ISBN: 0-9768976-1-X

Cover Art by Ardy Scott
Caricatoon of Margaret Searles by James Oddie

PRINTED IN THE UNITED STATES OF AMERICA.

DEDICATION

For all the brave, wonderful Brits, especially those I was lucky enough to meet on my travels.

When I had to leave England, like Margaret Millet, I sat in Heathrow Airport and wept. No more Devonshire Cream.

FOREWORD

DEVONSHIRE CREAM is the chronicle of a dream come true. The reader should be warned that, while a murder mystery is mixed up in the story, that mystery is incidental. For Mrs. Millet and Mrs. Hark, the excitement and peril of solving a nearly perfect crime is only the frosting (the cream?) on their English adventure.

At the time of this story, Margaret Millet has been alone (happily divorced) for years. Her daughter is grown, and she gets by on the income from her rental cottages in Brinyside, Oregon. She gets by, but that's all. So when a windfall of cash comes her way, you'd think she'd hang on to the money, wouldn't you? That would be the sensible, timid thing to do.

And she is sensible but timid? Not she. This may be the only chance she will ever have to realize her dream. All her life, she has longed to visit England, the home of her ancestors. She has read and loved Marjorie Sharp, Dornford Yates, Noel Coward, Muriel Spark, and Agatha Christie. This is her chance to see all the places she's read about and meet some real English people for herself. Her dearest friend, Judy Hark, is delighted to join her for the trip.

CAST OF CHARACTERS

Mrs. Margaret Millet... All her life she's wanted to visit England, the home of her ancestors. An unexpected windfall makes it possible.

Mrs. Judith Hark... Mrs. Millet's elegant friend loves to travel, is delighted to come along.

Sybil Darington... A lady of her class and beauty shouldn't have to work, but this one guides tours since her black sheep brother brought her family to ruin.

Richard Darington... Sybil's brother. Perhaps not as black and woolly as he might seem, but definitely a fool.

Malcolm Trewbridge... Drives the tour bus the way a Ship's Captain pilots a cruise. Would do anything for Sybil, and maybe he has.

Tony Budge... An ordinary postal clerk from St. Louis. Or is he?

Freddie Factor... A New York accountant of uncertain ethics. Good at juggling taxes, but tries to blackmail the wrong party.

Goldy Greening... Flamboyant woman of business with a dossier at Scotland Yard. Where did she get all those diamonds?

Grunt Davis... Goldy's companion and bodyguard.

Jake and Molly Arvin... The couple from Pasadena. Jake's video camera hides his fanatical green eyes, and Molly is dying for a cigarette.

Victor and Vicky Quist... wear matching outfits and own a dress shop in Virginia. Into fitness, money, and each other.

Inspector Christopher Lamb... called in from Scotland Yard. Is his judgement skewed by an attraction to Sybil Darington?

Chief Inspector Nail... of the Penzance Police. Knows he is over his head, but a British bulldog to the last.

Sir Augustus Cromarth... His fabulous collection of jewels is stolen, and he wants it back with interest.

Chapter 1
Mrs. Millet: Money and Roots

When thirteen thousand and some odd dollars dropped into Margaret Millet's lap all in one piece, some private devil in the under side of her brain began to prod. She knew perfectly well where the money should go, but the prodding wouldn't let her alone.

The check had come in the mail, in a long, fancy envelope from the Great Home Bank. Curious, she opened it right there in the post office. Surprise, surprise! The people who bought her former home had paid off the second mortgage she carried, and here was all that money at once! In a daze, she walked down the block to her bank and deposited the check—it wasn't something she wanted to carry around in her purse.

And now she sat at the table in her tiny apartment with the deposit receipt in one age speckled hand, while her demon prodded. "When will you ever have a chunk of money like this again?" it demanded. "It's now or never, you know."

Margaret ran the other hand through her short, gray-and-beige hair and gazed absently out the window, scarcely seeing the neat lawn and well weeded flower beds of her daughter's back yard.

Selling her house and remodeling Laura's garage into this cozy "granny pad" had worked out well, especially since she spent six months of the year elsewhere; in Brinyside, Oregon, running the four little beach cottages that were her main source of income.

She had a studio apartment there, too, and loved Brinyside in the summer, but in winter the wet, dark coast of Oregon was scarcely habitable. Her real home was here in Gambol Beach, California. Yes, it was an excellent arrangement.

Still, since her early teens, with a deep buried desire she had never seriously hoped to satisfy, she had longed to see another place. That was what her private devil was "on" about. He said, "Now! You can do it now!" and maliciously added, "You're not getting any younger, you know."

Finally she drew a deep breath and picked up the telephone. If her good friend Judy Hark could go with her, she'd do it. If not, not. Let the fates decide.

"Judy, it's Margaret. You'll never guess what's happened—I'm rich! Thirteen thousand dollars. The Stovers refinanced the house and paid off my second mortgage."

"That's wonderful," Judy responded. "What are you going to do with it, buy a new pickup?"

"No. I should apply it to my Oregon mortgage. I will apply ten thousand of it, but there's something I'd like to do with the rest ... if you're interested."

"If I'm interested—what do you mean?"

"Well, I thought we might go to England."

There, it was out. Margaret squirmed on the edge of her chair, her gray eyes squeezed shut, her plump body rigid, willing Judy to say "yes."

"What a wonderful idea! Have you heard from Bob Tyler? We could visit him in Yorkshire."

"You mean you'll go? Marvelous! No, I haven't heard from Bob in ages. I think he must have married Celia. But I'll write and tell him we're coming." How like Judy to assume she wanted to go to England to see Bob Tyler! Bob was English. They had met him at an RV park in Texas the previous winter, "doing America" in his motorhome. Margaret Millet, long divorced and happily single, was attracted, but Bob had a woman friend in England. In spite of Judy's best match-making, the friendship had remained platonic.

Judy said, "Let me talk it over with Willy. How long would we be gone? I haven't taken a trip in ages; I'm sure he won't mind."

"Mind? He should come! Tell him I'd love it if he came along. I'll have to see what it costs, but I'd like to stay three weeks, if I can afford it." Where did that come from? Margaret was amazed to find a full blown trip plan in her mind. Evidently, her devil had been busy.

She added, "We can't go until fall of course, because I have to run my cottages in Oregon this summer, but fall's the best time, anyway. The theater season in London! Just think—all the new plays and musicals—the best in the world! I especially want to see *The Mousetrap* before it closes. I don't know about Yorkshire, but I've always wanted to visit the south coast—Devonshire and Cornwall. That's where my ancestors came from."

"*The Mousetrap*! Isn't that a murder mystery?" Judy laughed, and could be heard telling Willy, "Yes, it's Margaret. Don't get excited, nobody's been murdered."

That was in March, and to seal the bargain with her devil, Margaret Millet immediately applied for a passport.

In May, she made her spring migration up the coast to Oregon. Business was good at the beach cottages that summer; "regulars" from Portland and Seattle and as far away as Montana came on vacation, bringing their children, their fishing gear, their surfboards, their friends. Margaret had rented out the cottages for six years now, and hardly needed to advertise in the Portland newspaper any more. People came back every year and sent their friends.

All summer, Margaret dreamed and planned and conferred with the best travel agent in Brinyside. As she scrubbed out bath tubs and toilets, she imagined walking down Drury Lane, the spiritual home of the young Alec Guinness and Stanley Holloway. As she vacuumed and dusted, she wondered if she could find Brittania Mews (Margery Sharp was her favorite author). As she weeded flowerbeds, she thought of her Penfold ancestors. Did the family still flourish in Devonshire and Cornwall? Could the name Penfold be found in English telephone directories? Was she really to find out?

Her travel agent said that three thousand dollars would buy a one week bus tour of the English West Country, from London to Land's End and back through Bath and Oxford, sight-seeing all the way. Plus a week in a small Bloomsbury hotel, near the London theater district. Plus a third week, which could be spent in Yorkshire, or any other place they chose. "That late in the season, you won't have any trouble with lodging, as long as you stay out of London. Just take your pick when you get there," the agent said.

Margaret pinched herself black and blue and began to realize it could happen. She would see England, just as she'd always dreamed.

It was lucky the vacation rental business was good; she'd have to buy new clothes. One couldn't tour England in blue jeans, tee shirts, and tennis shoes—especially not in the company of Judy Hark, that elegant, slender fashion plate whose perfectly styled auburn hair had never turned gray, whose make up was always flawless, who wore high heels by choice. Margaret Millet never revealed her age, but her fiftieth birthday present to herself had been to throw away all her high heeled shoes.

The summer passed. Vacationers went home, and Margaret's real estate agent supplied monthly renters for the winter. A last flurry of telephone calls to California; Laura and Tiny, her daughter and son in law, wished her *bon voyage*, and Judy said, "I'll meet you at the Pan Am ticket counter in Seattle. My flight gets in at 5:00 P.M."

A large suitcase and a carry on were stuffed to bursting. One more night to get through—she'd never be able to sleep! Then the alarm clock rang madly in her ear, and the traveling began; A bus to Portland, a plane to Seattle.

The trans polar flight, Seattle to London, was uneventful and didn't even seem long, as Margaret and Judy had a whole summer to catch up on. When the huge plane shuddered in rough air, the pilot, who chatted frequently on the cabin loudspeaker, said, "There's some of that unexpected turbulence we were expecting." They lost eight hours due to time zones and got no sleep.

At Heathrow, a red suited girl with a clipboard stood just past customs, calling "Gateway World passengers, this way, please." Margaret and Judy joined her flock, gave her their baggage checks, and trailed along to a waiting bus for the ride into London.

Both in a trance like state, past sleepy, they balanced on the edge of exhaustion. It was late afternoon, London time, and the guide spoke of a river boat excursion on the Thames that evening.

Judy said, "All I want is a bowl of soup and a bed that doesn't move."

Margaret, groggy but rapturous, gazed out the window at England and said, "I'm with you."

London was having a warm, muggy day with a gray overcast that threatened rain. Un-airconditioned, the bus soon smelled of the rumpled, sweaty travelers who shifted in their seats, removing jackets and coats. Judy, a born people watcher, observed her fellow tourists, while Margaret looked out the window at England. Yes, England; she was truly here, at last, on English soil.

Still in the outskirts of the city, the bus dove down into the bowels of a large hotel. The passengers checked in at a special registration counter and were elevated with carts of luggage to the small, anonymous cells of a typical European "bed factory."

"I wonder if any of those people on the bus will be on our tour," Judy said. "Did you see the couple with the video camera? He taped the airport tunnels, even. And she sure hated to put out her cigarette. Lit another as soon as she got off the bus." Judy sat tentatively on the nearest bed, bounced a little, and collapsed full length with a sigh. "I'm exhausted! We ought to eat I suppose, but I couldn't go down without a shower and clean clothes. Shall we order something from room service?"

Margaret tossed her jacket on the other bed and examined the cards and brochures on the dresser. "Here's a room service menu. You choose, Judy, and I'll have the same." She eased off her shoes and opened her small case.

Judy picked up the menu. "How about some cottage pie? 'Garden vegetables topped with mash and oven-browned.' Topped with mash—what does that mean?"

Margaret dug out her robe and slippers. How lovely to shed the clothes she'd been wearing for nearly twenty four hours! "Mashed potatoes, I think. As in 'bangers and mash.' Sounds good." English and American were not the same language, she knew. Her addiction to English authors was a help, already.

Chapter 2
Mrs. Hark: The Tan Man

Judy Hark fumbled for the bedside telephone and stilled its insistent buzz, mumbling "Hblmum" into the receiver.

"Six o'clock, Mum. Are we awake now?" said a cheery voice. "That's it, then. Six o'clock. Don't go off again, now, or you'll miss the tour."

The tour. London. "Thank you, I'm awake." She stretched to replace the phone. The single narrow window was still black, but the transom admitted a pale glow from the hall. Propping herself on one elbow, she looked at Margaret, stirring in the other bed. Let her rest, she thought. She doesn't wear any makeup but lipstick, and only needs to run a comb through that shag haircut.

Judy rose and stepped into the bathroom to don a summery print dress, use her curling iron with its European voltage adaptor, and put on her morning face. When she emerged, every auburn curl in place, Margaret was up and dressed.

"You look perfectly elegant," Judy approved. "I haven't seen that red jacket before—is it new?" How nice to see Margaret minding her appearance. Though slightly overweight, she had a pretty face even without make up.

Margaret packed the red canvas tote bag furnished by Gateway World Tours. "Should I put an extra blouse in here or leave it in the suitcase?"

"The suitcase." Judy pinned on an enameled brooch purchased in Italy two years before. She and Willy could afford to travel. She had cruised Alaska, the Caribbean, and Hawaii, and toured Spain, Morocco, and Italy. Willy used to go with her, but lately he preferred to stay home and let her travel with friends.

She set their suitcases in the hall for pick up and said, "As soon as you're ready, Margaret? Let's try the 'English Breakfast Included.' I'm starved."

"English Breakfast Included" was quite a spread. Porridge (oatmeal mush), eggs, English bacon (lean, tender meat, more like sugar cured ham than American bacon), sausages (the filling ground cornmeal fine) and grilled tomato halves, with coffee or tea. They served themselves, cafeteria style.

"I never eat this much breakfast," Judy said. "We'll put on weight if we're not careful."

Margaret forked in another mouthful of bacon. "But it's... let's see... eleven o'clock at night, at home. No wonder we're hungry. Don't think of it as breakfast."

A waitress brought tea on a tray; a silver plated pot of tea bags in boiling water, another pot of plain hot water, and a pitcher of hot milk. Margaret, the tea drinker, added hot water as the tea grew stronger, and drank cup after cup.

The behemoth tour bus waited in the hotel's underground garage, its motor politely rumbling. Tourists milled around their guide, young and fair in Gateway World's smartly tailored red suit. She's lovely, Judy thought as she got closer. The nose of a plastic surgeon's dreams. Still in her twenties? Late twenties, to have that much poise. What perfect skin—and honey colored hair—a beauty, no less.

"West Country Tour here," the guide said in a sweet, high voice, the accent decidedly upper class (Professor Higgins would have approved). "I'm Sybil Darington, and I'll be with you all the way. Just give me your names and take any seats you like—we'll rotate each day, to be fair to everyone. Where are the singles?" She stretched to look for strays and moved toward the bus.

Judy chose a seat on the left hand side, about half way back in the bus. "You take the window, Margaret. I'm taller. I can see over you."

A round, medium sized man in tan took the window seat in front of Margaret. He wore a tan twill jacket, tan canvas hat, suntan pants, and carried a small tan satchel which he placed beside him on the seat. Judy's eyes passed over him, noting his round, ordinary face, thinning tan hair, and pale tan eyes, and she dismissed him as inconsequential and too young for Margaret Millet, anyway.

Everyone else entered two by two, like boarding the ark. The trim, athletic-looking pair across the aisle even wore matched red shirts, leaving no doubt of their couplehood. In their early fifties? They probably jogged together every morning before going to their respective career jobs.

Yes, there was the man with the video camera, taping the inside of the bus. Judy smiled and waved, so the folks at home could see the tour group was one big happy party. You're welcome, she nodded. Always glad to oblige.

Oh, my. She nudged Margaret and nodded toward a woman near the front of the bus. Indeed, the woman was gaudy. Her raiment—the only possible word—seemed to be mostly flowing purple scarves, accented by glittering jeweled pins. Large in all directions, she and the man sitting next to her (he looked more like a wrestler than a man who would buy diamonds) filled the seat like two loaves of bread, raised and baked in one pan.

"Look at that, Margaret. Right up front. The orange hair and diamonds."

"Oh, Judy—I see what you mean."

Sybil Darington glided along the aisle with her clipboard and stopped beside the tan man. "Mr. Factor?"

"No. I'm Tony Budge. I paid the single supplement."

"Yes, Mr. Budge. That's for private hotel rooms," she explained tactfully. "We have another single who'll share the bus seat with you—the tour is fully booked, forty-eight seats, forty-eight passengers. Where is he, I wonder?" She peered out the window.

Judy smiled. This must be the missing single, now—a wiry little man charging across the garage, his Gateway World tote bag held high like a banner. He bounced into the bus, took a step or two down the aisle, and stopped dead at the sight of Sybil in her red suit. His jaw dropped, revealing long lower teeth, white against his swarthy skin.

"Well, good morning Gorjus! Sorry, I overslept—wow! I'm really sorry!"

Apparently, Sybil was used to the effect she had on males. She rose above the bumptious greeting with a frosty smile. "Mr. Factor? This is Mr. Budge. You'll share a seat in the bus."

"You can call me Freddie—please call me Freddie!" he pleaded, unsquelched. Then he turned to Tony Budge. "Can I stow that satchel for you, buddy?"

Freddie reached for the satchel, only to have it snatched away. Budge put it on his lap, and seemed none too happy to share the seat.

Judy inspected Freddie's curly, black hair, long at the nape, and his foxy profile as he stowed the red tote-bag overhead and dropped into the seat in front of her. Sybil had coped skillfully with these men, she thought. Her startling beauty was offset by dignity and breeding.

A blast of Freddie Factor's cologne reached her. "Can you open the window, Margaret? British Tannery!" she whispered.

Margaret sniffed and wrinkled her nose in distaste. "Ugh... no, it doesn't open." She twisted the air conditioning nozzle. "Yes, that's better." Cool air rushed over them, driving the sickening, musky smell away.

Judy Hark was not the only person who scanned the passengers. Someone else took an intense interest. Someone else did not dismiss the tan man as inconsequential. This watcher thought, there he is; that's the man. How perfectly anonymous. He disappears while you look at him, like a single fly on a busy dung hill, showing no mark to set him off from the swarm. Handle this right and I'm set for life. Tony Budge? No one will miss him.

Sybil, satisfied with her passenger count, went forward to her station beside the driver and picked up the microphone. "Good morning all! I hope you had a delightful evening in London and feel ready for today's adventures! But first I want you to meet our driver, Malcolm. Our entire trip, I'm sure you'll all agree, depends upon the skill and judgement of our bus driver—a Very Important Person—who gets little recognition, you know. We all tend to take him for granted. Malcolm has a fine record; eight years of safe driving. So every morning, we're going to give him a rousing welcome to show how much we appreciate him."

She smiled her dazzling smile at each passenger in turn. Each passenger smiled back, stopped talking, and gave his or her entire attention. It was nice to watch. "Please stand up, Malcolm, and let us have a look at you."

The driver, almost military in his tailored gray uniform, unfolded himself from under the wheel and stood beside Sybil for inspection. A sturdy six footer, he doffed his billed cap, revealing thick, dark hair and a prominent brow.

"Now, all together, please, nice and loud. Good Morning, Malcolm!"

Straggly and weak, a little embarrassed, the passengers responded, "Good Morning, Malcolm."

Hand cupped to ear, Sybil sang, "I can't hear you! You've got to do better—that won't wake him up! Again!"

"Good Morning, MALCOLM." And then, finally getting into the spirit of the thing, "GOOD MORNING, MALCOLM!" A burst of good humored laughter started the day.

The bus swayed out into the streets. After a series of twists and turns, it entered a thru way and sped along the raised roadbed through the suburban neighborhoods of London. The houses and apartment buildings were of stone or brick; sturdy, permanent. The streets were paved with blocks of stone.

"So different," Margaret said. "Built to last." They passed an area of tall brick row-houses with small gardens front and rear. Although joined at the sides, they were not alike. Each roof was different; some of gray slates, some tiled, some asphalt-shingled. Each house was trimmed to suit its owner, each front garden expressed individual taste and effort.

"Like the row houses south of San Francisco, except no stucco," Judy said. "Wonder how old they are?"

"The trees look old," Margaret said. "What would it be like to live where they don't tear things down and start over every few years?"

"Nothing like California."

Traffic thinned, and the driver picked up the microphone. Malcolm sounded as English as Sybil but in a different way. More like Bob Tyler, Judy thought. Wonder if he's from Yorkshire, too?

"Many of you come from countries where they drive on the wrong side of the road," Malcolm told them. "In case you thought that was the right side of the road, I'd just like to explain why the right side is... uhmm... the wrong side, if you see wot I mean.

"It all started in the 'Days of Chivalry.' Our roads go back to the Knights on horseback. Well, unless he's left handed, your Knight rides a horse with the reins in his left hand and keeps his right hand free for his sword. And he rides on the left side of the road so he can use that sword, if he meets a wrong un coomin' the other way. Now then, that explains it, doesn't it? You can go home and tell the folks why they're driving on the wrong side, can't you?"

Laughter followed these remarks, and Judy said, "It makes sense. Wonder how it got turned around?"

London suburbs yielded to the orchards and hop fields of Kent. A mist began to fall, then turned to a gentle, soaking rain. The bus skirted Canterbury's medieval walls, built of round, high piled stones with concrete blocks reinforcing the corners; the latter a modern addition. They turned on a narrow, cobblestone street and came to rest in a car park near their first stop, Canterbury Cathedral, England's Mother Church and Bishopric of the ill fated Thomas Becket.

"We're sorry, since it's Sunday and church services are being held, we can't go inside the Cathedral," Sybil told them. She went on to describe some of what they would miss; the copper gilt effigy of Edward the Black Prince in full armor, and rows of twelfth century stained glass windows. Under a black umbrella, she led them through Christ Church Gate, her three inch heels clacking on the pavements.

Judy should have known better, but she hadn't brought an umbrella. Margaret had and was willing to share, after she got it open. By the time they had admired the cathedral as a whole and peered through a side door at a tiny portion of the interior, Judy was quite damp and had cold, wet feet.

The stop was brief. The smokers did, the photographers took pictures, the video camera man inspected the scene through his lens and saw nothing with his own eyes. Then Sybil cajoled them back to the bus, saying they had a long way to go, and the really fascinating feature of the day was in Portsmouth, where they would visit HMS Victory, Admiral Nelson's last ship. "And we want to get there with plenty of time in hand."

The tan man took pictures with an intricate, expensive looking camera. He stopped outside the bus door to stow it back in his satchel, then squeezed back into line just ahead of Judy Hark. As he got on, a scrap of yellow paper, like a bit of wrapping from a package of film, fluttered down and landed in the lap of the gaudy, orange-haired woman. Judy saw it fall, but thought nothing of it, as she squeezed around people stowing wet umbrellas and raincoats in the racks overhead. If the paper was anything but a bit of trash, the woman would have said something instead of crumpling it in one diamond-encrusted hand.

Chapter 3
Mrs. Millet: Fellow Tourists

A lifelong ocean lover, Margaret Millet looked forward to Brighton, the first beach town on their itinerary. When the bus stopped, however, Sybil again stressed the need for haste, before letting them off. "I wish we could give you more time in this famous old seaside resort, but we must make Portsmouth before HMS Victory closes down for the night. It's really a highlight of the trip and well worth the rush." She lifted a lock of her honey colored hair and tucked it behind her ear. "Malcolm is going for petrol. The bus will be back in this same spot in one hour, so find a restaurant nearby, and please, don't be late."

Standing aside, Sybil gently hustled her flock off the bus, then drove away with Malcolm. The flock clucked and squawked and scattered to seek food, like chickens turned loose in an orchard.

"Brighton," Margaret said reverently. "What a shame we can't stroll down the seafront and take it in. Prince Edward made it famous—oh, I'd love to walk around and see it!"

"We'd better walk around and find some food," Judy said. "At least, it's stopped raining." Taking Margaret's arm, she moved toward the nearest eating establishment.

This proved to be full, with a rapidly lengthening line outside. "No hope. Let's go across the street."

On the third try, they entered a small, grubby cafe with no waiting line. No empty tables, but two chairs were vacant at a table for four. Judy smiled sweetly, said "Do you mind?" and sat down without waiting for a reply.

Two men in coveralls moved their plates closer together, cheerfully making room.

"Thank you," Margaret said. "We're on a tour and only have an hour for lunch."

"Only forty-five minutes, now." Judy waved to catch the waitress's eye.

Judy is never ignored in restaurants, Margaret thought. It's because she looks like Somebody. They ordered sandwiches and soup and were promptly served, even though others around them were waiting.

"American ladies, aren't yer?" asked one of the men. "Where y' headed?"

"Portsmouth, tonight," Margaret said between bites. "Then on to Devon and Cornwall."

"Portsmouth—aye, I was there durin' the war," the man said. "All bombed to blazes, it was. Got a turrible poundin' from the Jerries, Portsmouth did." The men paid their tab and went out, leaving the ladies in sole possession of the table.

Thinking of Canterbury, Margaret said, "My first Cathedral, and I only got a peek inside. Wonderful old walls, though—the city walls, I mean—to have stood all this time. What a sense of history in a place like that! My ancestors were an ancient race."

"As cathedrals go, Canterbury's not exceptional," Judy said. "What do you think of that young man in front of us on the bus? Is he going to give our guide a bad time?"

"Freddie? I think she can handle him." Margaret willingly abandoned cathedrals for people. "What was his last name—Factor? Bet he changed it from Factolini or something. Younger than most of the group, too—wonder why he's on a tour like this, all by himself?"

"He looks and sounds like a small time New York gangster," Judy said. Freddie's bumptiousness annoyed her.

"You're right. Maybe he had to get out of town." Margaret chuckled, downed the last bite of her sandwich and reached for her purse. "Let's get back to the bus. It's a shame not to see more of Brighton, but I hate to be a straggler."

Portsmouth is a navy town, with ships at anchor in the harbor. It reminded Margaret of Seattle, where she had lived in the early days of her marriage. The first sight of HMS Victory moored broadside to the wharf, with three decks of black cannon bristling through her gun ports, made her catch her breath. "Imagine being on a wooden ship, looking into those guns!"

The tourists mounted a steep gangplank to the second deck, where a detail of British sailors met them, split them into groups of six, and steered the groups in different directions about the ship. Margaret and Judy found themselves grouped with two Australian schoolteachers, the video nut, and his nicotine addicted wife.

"I'm Molly Arvin, and this is Jake. Is it okay to smoke, do you suppose?" Molly's harsh, gravelly voice was as deep as a man's.

Margaret pointed to a prominent "NO SMOKING" sign, and said, "It's a wooden ship." What an International Incident, if an American tourist set fire to the Victory!

She got a good look at Jake Arvin (the first time his face had not been obscured by his camera) when they climbed to the upper deck. Incredibly steep, the stairs had treads four inches wide and risers a foot high. Even Jake had to look where he was going and hold the handrail.

He had a fanatic's eyes, large, almond shaped, and green—startling in his narrow, sun-tanned face. He tucked the camera under one arm to clamber up the stair, and at the top, pulled a midget tape recorder from his pocket, turned it on, and aimed it toward their sailor guide.

"We regard this station as a post of honor in Her Majesty's Navy," the British Tar said. "Admiral Lord Nelson, our Naval Hero, died on this ship, fatally wounded by a sniper during the battle of Trafalgar in 1805." A likeable fellow, curly haired and upright in his uniform, he seemed extremely fit and agile. Must be from scrambling up and down this ship all day, Margaret decided, panting from the climb.

The sailor showed them the space around a cannon, about the size of a jail cell, in which a full gun crew lived, ate, and slept in hammocks, in the days of Horatio Nelson. Then he led them down three sets of those cliff-like stairs to the Surgeon's Deck and pointed out the spot where Nelson died, after learning that England had won the battle.

"When Nelson was dying, he said, 'Thank God, I have done my duty,' His last words were to his friend and fellow officer. He said, 'Kiss me, Hardy.' and died on this spot."

Molly Arvin had plenty of time to smoke while the tour reassembled on the wharf.

Now that the objectives of the day were met, Sybil relaxed noticeably. She sat up front beside Malcolm during the ride to the hotel. Watching them, Margaret enjoyed the way Malcolm deftly handled the bus, while dropping comments from the side of his mouth that made Sybil laugh—probably comments on the members of the tour.

The Harbor Hotel looked across the street to the Portsmouth Pier. The tour group used a private dining room and, as on the Victory, was seated in groups of six, at round tables with glistening china, white linen, and red napkins folded into gay cockades.

Margaret and Judy took a vacant table, and waited to see who their dinner companions would be.

"We meet again! May we join you?" Molly Arvin, glamorous in an ivory cocktail dress. Jake stood behind her with his camera, taping the dining room and adjoining bar.

"Yes, of course," Judy said. "Tell me about yourselves. You're from Pasadena, didn't you say? We're from California, too." She wore a black one piece garment far too elegant to be called a jump-suit, with earrings and bracelet of carved silver beads.

Her auburn hair, upswept with the aid of the curling iron, billowed in ringlets on top of her head. A pleasant, get-acquainted conversation began, one socialite to another.

Jake Arvin stowed his camera under a chair and produced a large map before he sat down. "I'm marking our route," he announced. "See, from London to Canterbury we went almost due East. Then we took A28 Southwest to Ashford and A259 to Hastings, '1066 and all that,' as Sybil said. Then Brighton for lunch, and on to Portsmouth. Arundel castle was right here..." he pointed to a spot on the map, "and I got a great zoom shot of it through the window of the bus—I panned from the passenger's faces, looking at it—a great shot."

He passed the map to Margaret so she could see the red ink tracing their route. It was headed "Tourist Route Series/ SOUTH ENGLAND AND WALES/Nine Miles per Inch." Doing an eyeball measurement and some mental arithmetic, Margaret estimated they had covered about 160 miles that day. "What a good idea," she said, stretching to hand it back. "And what a wonderful record you'll have of the trip!"

"The camera? Yes, we like to watch the tapes afterward, when we're back home."

"Don't be modest, Jake. You know everyone says you should market them as travelogues, they're so good," Molly said. "He keeps a notebook too, so he'll know what everything is and when we were there."

"And I record on audio tape—like at the ship today." Jake pushed the small ashtray at his place toward Molly, who had already filled her own.

Margaret smelled cologne mixed with Molly's smoke before she saw Freddie Factor. He pulled out the chair next to Jake's, bumped it against the wall behind him and cast a searching eye around the dining room as he sat down. He hadn't changed and still wore the loud sport coat, open shirt, and heavy gold neck chain that had prompted Judy's remark about petty gangsters.

"Be careful, taking pictures," Freddie said. "You don't know who's traveling with who." His leer said this was a joke. "Greetings, Ladies. Where's our beautchus English Rose?"

"Taking the evening off, I expect," Judy snapped. "She has a lot to put up with, poor girl. I hope she's enjoying herself."

"Whoo oo, excuse me!" Freddie made a silly flapping gesture with his hand and turned to Jake, the other male at the table, with a shrug. "What's to eat in this joint?" he asked.

Bowls of mashed potato and mixed vegetables, a platter of roast lamb, and individual fruit salads were served. Everyone had a full plate before the last seat at the table was occupied. In fact, it was the last empty place in the room, or the tan man might have sat elsewhere. If he had not enjoyed being paired with Freddie on the bus, he liked it even less at the table; Margaret could see the annoyance in his face as he pulled out the chair.

"...and this tour always starts on a Sunday, according to the brochure," Jake Arvin was saying. "So they always get to Canterbury on Sunday, there are always church services, and nobody ever gets to see the inside of the Cathedral—you see? And our guide was so apologetic, made it sound like something unusual. They never get inside!"

Tony Budge sat down and said, "We'll see the cathedral in Salisbury, I think. That's day three, before Stonehenge. There are always trade-offs when you take a tour like this. So much ground to cover, and so little time." He scooted his chair closer to Margaret (and farther from Freddie), and put his tan satchel between his feet.

"Sounds like you travel a lot," Margaret said, passing him the peas and carrots.

His smile revealed small, even teeth, relieving the plainness of his round face. "It's my passion," he said, simply. "I work at the St. Louis Post Office and get five weeks of vacation a year. When I get home from one trip, I start planning the next."

"How wonderful! I've never been outside the U.S. much, until now. Well, Canada and Mexico, and I did take a Caribbean cruise once... Judy's been all over the world, though. You've probably seen some of the same places."

Budge pulled his passport from the inside pocket of his tan jacket and passed it to Judy. "Have you ever been to Tanzania?" he asked, pointing to a visa stamp on the last page. "I'm forty seven. When I retire at fifty five, I'll have visited every country on the map that's open to Americans."

His voice was quiet, ordinary, unboastful. He simply stated the facts. Margaret was touched by the thought that this might be all the man had. His claim to fame. He might have no personal life whatever, poor fellow, other than his solitary travels.

Chapter 4
Mrs. Hark: The Portsmouth Pub

Back in their fifth floor room after dinner, Judy Hark was not ready to call it a day. She was tired but after eight hours on a bus, she needed movement and relaxation. "I'm glad you like it," she replied to Margaret"s compliments on her black outfit. "I like it myself, and I think it deserves to see Portsmouth.

"That's pretty too," she fingered Margaret's soft pullover of red boucle, with a golden thread woven into the fabric. Margaret's travel wardrobe showed unusual attention, for Margaret. Judy approved. "The red is so good with your tan. Did you spend lots of time on the beach this summer?"

"All my clothes for the trip are red, white, and blue," Margaret said. "They're British colors, too, you know. Oh, Judy, I don't remember what I did in Brinyside this summer—I imagined England the whole time. And now I'm here! I can't believe it. Yes, let's go look at Portsmouth!"

Freddie Factor's Brooklyn accent could be heard above the din in the hotel bar. Judy grimaced, Margaret winced, and they turned away, pushing through the heavy glass entrance doors.

Across the well-lit street, the Portsmouth Pier was gated and dark, probably for the season. Fresh salt air made Judy glad of her quilted jacket, and she wondered if Margaret's sweater was warm enough. She struck out briskly down the street, turned a corner, and spotted a sign that said "PUB." Margaret hustled to keep up.

Housed in a narrow structure of square and ancient stones, the pub glowed with English oak and diamond paned amber windows, under massive beams. Fresh air from an up-to-date air conditioning system diluted the smells of beer and tobacco—the atmosphere was quite breathable—and a genial clamor of laughter and talk filled the room, pushing loneliness and solitude outside. A friendly, cozy place.

Judy led the way to a corner table. When her eyes adjusted to the dim lighting, she looked for waiters, but drinks were dispensed at the bar. "What shall I ask for, Margaret? I don't know the names of any English beers."

"Let's see," said the England expert, "beer and ale come in pints or half-pints. I recommend the half. And I think, to get the kind of light beer we're used to, we ask for lager. 'A half of lager,' that should do it. I'll go." Margaret slung her purse over her shoulder and headed for the bar.

"Aren't you on the tour?" A woman at the next table leaned toward Judy. The female half of the matched set. The male half sat beside her and, instead of red shirts, they now wore white sweaters with stylized silver monograms.

This pair had seemed unapproachable in their unity, and Judy was glad the woman spoke to her, instead of the other way around. She liked knowing her tour companions; it was much more fun if everybody made friends. Beaming, she scooted the tray-sized table closer to theirs and was able to introduce her new acquaintances when Margaret returned.

"Margaret Millet, Victor and Vicky Quist. Remember them on the bus? They're from Virginia."

Margaret smiled and nodded, carefully placing two large, brimful glasses on the table. "It's not cold—and not Terlingua Ale, I'm afraid."

"Hardly anything is," Judy said. "We got Terlingua Ale in Texas," she explained to the Quists. "It's a local brew, down in the Big Bend Country. Really good." She took a tentative sip from her glass.

"Barbaric, the way they serve it warm," Victor Quist said. "What do you think of the tour, so far?"

Margaret said, "I love it. The whole country seems so permanent—so lasting. Everything looks like it was built centuries ago, and is still in use."

"This place certainly looks old," Judy said. "Oh, look, there's Diamond Lil!"

The Quists turned in a single motion, like Siamese twins, and laughed. "That's Goldy Greening," Victor said. "She toured the Victory with us. Caused quite a stir waving all those jewels around—our sailor was goggle-eyed."

"And dutiful! 'Yes, Mum, No, Mum, Can I help you up the stairs, Mum.' Almost ruined my notion of sturdy British independence," Vicky giggled. "He didn't know what to do with her when she wouldn't climb down to the lower deck. She plopped down on a coil of rope and refused to move. He was frantic 'til another sailor offered to stay with her."

"They can't leave anybody wandering around by themselves, I guess. I see the bodyguard's here, too." Victor indicated Goldy Greening's large companion.

"The bodyguard? You mean he's not her husband?" Judy asked.

"Oh, no. We all said our names you know, and she said, 'I'm Goldy Greening, and this is Davis, my bodyguard,' all the time flashing those sparklers. The poor man never uttered a word."

"Where's she from? Do you know?"

"She didn't say. Sounds English, but not like Sybil. More like a sales clerk in one of the shops. That's why it seemed so funny, the sailor bowing and scraping. He was just impressed by the jewelry."

"No," Victor said. "She's got more than diamonds. She's got authority. She's the boss!"

"I'd love to get her in the shop," Vicky said. "Remember that peacock blue caftan with the draped neck?"

"Yes, perfect."

"Oh, do you have a dress shop?" Judy was all ears.

Vicky nodded. "But the diamonds wouldn't do with that caftan. A long rope of pearls, I think."

Goldy Greening advanced into the pub like an ocean liner putting to sea, and the crowd parted before her. She chose a table in the center of the room, and Davis fetched two foaming pints from the bar. Goldy raised her mug to the pub at large and drank deeply, then produced a diamond studded cigarette holder. Davis solemnly lit her cigarette with a diamond studded lighter.

"I think they're fakes," Margaret said. "Sorry, but I just don't believe in those diamonds."

"What a cynic," Judy chided. "Why would she need a bodyguard, if they're not real?"

"Why, indeed?" Margaret smiled a crooked smile.

Goldy tilted her face upward and wiped under each mascaraed eye with a dainty square of linen and lace—a gesture they would often see in the days to come. She waved the handkerchief flirtatiously at the nearest male, a moustached gent quaffing his pint at the next table. He spluttered with delight and had to be slapped on the back by his pals. Heavily made up, Goldy's long false lashes hid small, beady eyes that missed nothing. Her large, flattish lips glistened with orange lipstick matched to the orange-red hair, and she had changed her purple draperies for lavender and black with a fox stole hanging carelessly from one shoulder. She was eminently at home in the pub.

The sailors and dock workers of Portsmouth became her jolly companions, flocking around her like seagulls being fed. Even the dart board went unused for half an hour.

Judy looked on, glad she had chosen a table in the farthest corner, while the Quists regaled her with the latest fashion news from Virginia Beach.

"It's a family business," Victor said. "I've worked in the store ever since I got out of college. Our heaviest trade comes in the summer, when the whole world goes to the beach—that's why we always take our vacation in the fall. We usually go to Maine, but this year..."

"We're combining pleasure with business," Vicky finished the sentence. "Some lovely new styles coming out of London these days, you know. After the tour, we'll go to some of the fashion shows."

Margaret, to whom fashion meant she could no longer get bell-bottom jeans, took small part in this discussion. She was even so rude as to interrupt it. "Why does that man look so familiar," she said, touching Judy's arm to get attention.

Judy, a little annoyed, turned to look. The group around Goldy and Davis had ebbed away. Only one man remained; a slender, handsome young fellow with fair hair and a fine profile. He and Goldy had their heads close together and seemed engaged in intense conversation.

Judy shrugged, "I don't know—is he on the tour?" She couldn't really see his face. Vicky said something about the new fall colors, and she turned to hear it.

"TIME! Last call, folks! Time!" The bartender bellowed, and there was a rush to the bar for one more pint before closing.

"Not for us, thanks," Victor said. The bottles in front of the Quists were labeled Ginger Ale. "We jog in the morning; care to join us?"

I knew they were joggers, Judy thought. "What time will you get up?"

"The Vics," as she mentally dubbed them, would rise at five o'clock to jog the streets of Portsmouth. Judy looked at Margaret who sagged with weariness at the thought, and declined.

In the hotel room, Judy removed her makeup, brushed her hair, and selected her clothes for the next day, while Margaret wrote copiously in her trip journal.

"Has Canterbury got an e or two u's?"

Judy spelled Canterbury and said, "We're beginning to know people, aren't we? The Arvins at dinner—did you like them?"

"Yes, but... addictive personalities, both of them." Margaret's mouth puckered in distaste. "I met someone with green eyes like that once. He used to ride the bus I took to work in Seattle... when I was single the first time." She bent back to her journal.

Judy waited for more of that story, and when it didn't come, she said, "I thought they were interesting. Do you suppose we could get copies of some of Jake's video tapes? He's certainly making the most of the photo opportunities. I wonder if he really enjoys the trip or waits for the movie."

Margaret smiled and looked up from her writing. "Those two single men are going to be right in front of us the whole trip. The man with the satchel—Tony Mudge—no, Budge, I think. He's what Yeats called a 'world besotted traveler.'"

Judy dismissed Tony Budge. "He's too young for you. A postal clerk. And 'Freddie,' as we are all supposed to call him, is a royal pain. Do you think we should try to change seats with someone?"

"Oh no—they might take offense. I do hope Freddie runs out of aftershave, though. Could we bribe the chambermaid to steal the bottle?"

Trust Margaret to make me laugh, Judy thought. She completed her ablutions and snuggled under the Harbor Hotel's downy comforter. After she turned off the bedside lamp, she continued to chat quietly. She thought of a wise and penetrating comment about Goldy Greening, but drifted off to sleep before the words could be properly assembled.

Chapter 5
Mrs. Millet: The Class System

Unrecorded details woke Margaret Millet at 4:30 A.M., and since Judy's head was covered by bed-clothes, she risked the bedside lamp to add them to her journal. After all, she might never be in Portsmouth, England, again. Her impressions of the city, Admiral Nelson's ship, and the friendly pub of the previous evening should not be lost.

After breakfast (Margaret limited herself to the oatmeal porridge) "Day Two" of the tour began. Sybil, Malcolm, and the huge, slab-sided tour bus waited at the curb.

Seat rotation caused a lot of good-natured confusion. "Port side three seats back; starboard three seats forward," Sybil directed. "That's right. Port is the left side as you face forward. Starboard is the side behind the driver." The driver's seat was on the "wrong" side for most of the tourists, so some were still muddled by these instructions, but eventually they settled and joined Sybil in a resounding greeting to the driver: "GOOD MORNING, MALCOLM!"

Margaret sat on the aisle, saying "It's only fair. I had the window yesterday." Since she and Judy had moved back and the Quists (in bright blue windbreakers today) had moved forward, they were now six rows apart. Jake and Molly Arvin were closer though, across the aisle and one seat back.

Freddie Factor took the window seat while he had the chance. Budge came running up the street and climbed aboard, thrusting his satchel down the aisle before him, and sitting abruptly as the bus lurched away from the curb.

Sybil, fresh and cheerful as the sunny morning, bubbled into her microphone, "Speaking of port and starboard sides, I'm sure you've all heard the expression, 'Posh.' Did you know that it comes from 'Port Out, Starboard Home?' That's right, when sailing between England and India, one tried to get a stateroom on the port side of the ship going out and the starboard side coming home so one always had a view of the passing coastline. These were the best cabins, so Posh became a word for luxury accommodations. Bit of news?" She smiled at her listeners; they nodded and smiled back.

Tony Budge didn't listen. He muttered, "I can't understand it," to no one in particular. "Nothing at the post office at all. They were supposed to send word... and I nearly missed the bus!" Still out of breath, he puffed and shook his head, scowling.

Margaret had excellent hearing. She leaned forward and said, "Were you expecting mail from home, Mr. Budge?"

Startled, he jerked around. "Oh, no... well, just a message from a friend. Someone I'm supposed to see, later in the trip. The English postal service is usually so good—I can't understand it. I left word to forward anything that comes." He turned away abruptly.

"That should be all right, then," Margaret said. Her curiosity was decidedly piqued. How could he visit anybody when the tour was so fully arranged? Well, maybe at one of the overnight stops. She stared at the back of his head, wondering what he was up to and why he seemed so agitated about it.

Budge getting himself noticed, curse him! the watcher thought. What's happened to the transfer? What if the fools blow it? That old biddy is the nosy kind, too. And her friend—wants to know everybody on the tour. Keep an eye on those two....

With great skill, Malcolm maneuvered the bus through traffic to the Southsea docks, where it fell in line and lumbered aboard a big red ferry. "Day Two" was to be a day of boat rides and stately homes; Osborne House on the Isle of Wight, and Broadlands, the home of the Mountbatten family. To reach the latter, they would drive through the New Forest, a place Margaret had read about and was eager to see.

Sybil again: "On your itinerary, you'll see that we were to stay in Southampton this evening, but due to the Southampton-to-Cowes Regatta, all the hotels there are filled. We'll be staying in Bournemouth instead; a beautiful resort town with a lovely beach. We're booked into the Royal Plaza, one of the finest hotels. Sorry about Southampton, but during the Regatta, it's the most dreadful crush! Bournemouth will be much better for us."

"Cowes!" Margaret exclaimed. "It's pronounced 'cows' just like a dairy herd—I've always wondered how to say it. Didn't one of Nevil Shute's characters keep a boat there?"

Jake Arvin had his map out, and showed her Cowes, on the Isle of Wight, and the ferry routes to and from the island. "We're scheduled to bypass Cowes and ferry back to the mainland from Yarmouth," he said.

After the ferry left the docks, Malcolm released them to the car deck, thumping with engine noise and swept by a brisk, salty breeze. Margaret made for a good viewpoint on the rail; Judy tied a gauzy scarf over her hairdo and followed. The wide waters of the Solent gleamed before them, peppered with small boats and ships of all kinds. Directly ahead, a Royal Navy ship, "HMS JUNEAU" lettered on its stern, steamed out of the port. Rolling into the trough of Juneau's wake, the ferry played follow the leader, letting the Navy navigate through the small-craft traffic.

When the Quists joined them, Judy picked up the acquaintance where she'd left it the night before. Margaret, however, began to regret her skimpy breakfast. That small bowl of porridge had seemed sufficient at the time, but now the sea air stirred her appetite.

"I wonder if we could get a little something," she shouted over the engine noise. "On the upper deck, maybe?" She peered at the superstructure above her.

Judy had eaten the full English breakfast, so she stayed with the Quists while Margaret climbed the vibrating iron stairs. The top cabin was quieter and warmer, with a snack bar and benches where passengers could enjoy the crossing, sheltered from the wind. Smells of tea and cinnamon rolls wafted her way, and she purchased some of each before looking about for an empty table. Or at least an empty chair; all the tables were occupied. There—Malcolm and Sybil sat by the window—perhaps they wouldn't mind sharing.

"Good morning. May I join you?" Margaret hesitated, a hot styrofoam cup in one hand, and a flabby paper plate tilting under the large cinnamon roll in the other.

"Of course!" Sybil's smile glowed briefly. "Take my chair; I was just going. Have to do some paperwork, I'm afraid. Mrs. Millet, isn't it? Are you enjoying the trip?"

How does she do it? Margaret thought. Forty-eight names, and she comes up with mine, just like that! She carefully set cup and plate on the table and stood back so the guide could rise.

As Sybil's slender figure moved away, Malcolm watched her wistfully. "A smasher, that. A right dazzler, isn't she?"

"She certainly is," Margaret agreed, taking a bite of her bun.

"Right out of the top drawer. A piece of the upper crust. But not for the likes of me..."

"Oh, Malcolm, why ever not? You're a fine man! Good looking and... and clean and decent, too. Any girl could be proud..." She was astonished at the strength of her feeling. She had watched Malcolm perform his duties and seen his kindness and patience with even the most querulous tourists. If this wasn't a highly superior young man, she had learned nothing about people in all her years of experience with the species.

"Aye, you Americans!" he said. "If only it were that simple. Sybil's going to marry rich; her family expects it. Her brother won't find an heiress—he's blotted his copybook—so it's up to her."

Blotted his copybook—a phrase right out of her English novels. Did they really say that or was he pulling her leg?

"You're not married, Malcolm?" A personal question, but he started it.

"Have been. No more. She got tired of staying home alone, I guess. There's my kiddie, though—Darla. She stays with me mum in Manchester, and I see her between trips." The smile that lit his generous features showed better than words how much the child meant to him. With a little encouragement, he recounted his daughter's accomplishments ("She can read like smoke, already!") and produced pictures; Darla, age seven, all legs and teeth and long, dark hair.

Taking a small notebook from his pocket, Malcolm jotted down the cost of his breakfast, then gathered up the litter on the table and rose. "Enjoyed talking to you, Mrs. Millet. We'll be docking soon; better finish your tea." And he was off with a jingle of keys.

Mrs. Millet thought the parkland around Osborne House, Queen Victoria's favorite residence, was the loveliest place she'd ever seen. Acres and acres of green lawn and ancient, widely spaced trees surrounded the massive stone mansion. One huge, spreading oak shaded an area larger than a city block.

Entering the mansion through a narrow side door, the tour group formed a shambling double file, led and followed by Osborne House staff members. On a carpeted, roped off walkway, they passed through a series of high ceilinged rooms, craning their necks, peering and exclaiming at the royal portraits, Victorian furniture, statuary, and art objects that stuffed every available space.

"Glad I don't have to do the dusting," Margaret commented.

The rooms were not as large as she'd expected them to be, and somehow it made the "royals" more human. Lovely big fireplaces, though, and needed; probably the only source of heat. The twin desks where Victoria and Albert had dealt with state papers looked sturdy and functional. Parliament's dispatch box was still displayed there.

One side of the house faced the Solent, but was not open to tourists. After a circuit through the display rooms, they were extruded through the front entrance and told to make themselves free of the grounds, and to meet back at the bus in half an hour.

"A good brisk walk is just what I need," Vicky Quist said, linking arms with her husband. They stepped out on a broad path through the parkland.

Margaret and Judy followed more slowly. The path led away from Osborne House toward the water, and looking back they could see a rambling terrace, sheltered between two wings of the house. Balconies and a roof-top "widow's walk" also faced the idyllic view.

"Do you suppose anybody uses it now? Does Queen Elizabeth ever come here?" Judy wondered.

"An awful waste if they don't. Anyhow, the staff people have a fabulous place to work," Margaret said.

Turning, she almost bumped into Tony Budge, bent over his open satchel, mating a fat telescopic lens to his camera. A few feet away, Jake Arvin perched on a stone block (a mounting block?), his video camera sweeping a slow, panoramic arc to include Osborne House, the huge, old trees and the maritime view, and finally, for scale, focusing on human figures—Margaret, Judy, and Tony Budge. Budge looked out from under his tan hat just as Jake pointed the camera his way. Immediately he turned his back and scuttled away, almost running to put a large tree between himself and Jake's lens—or so it looked to Margaret Millet. How odd!

Farther along, a low fence edged a wide, grassy bridle path.

Three riders in jodhpurs and derby hats galloped past, part of an elite world of ease and luxury Margaret could barely imagine—and envied not at all.

"Simplify, simplify, simplify," she said softly. "What do you think, Judy? Shall we start back to the bus?"

"I suppose so. But I'd rather sit on that terrace and have Jeeves bring out the champagne..." Judy Hark could use any amount of ease and luxury.

They angled off through a hazel grove on a narrow walk that forced them into single file. Margaret picked up a fallen hazel leaf, admired its dainty, deckled edge and fine tracery of veins, and tucked it into her pocket calendar for a keepsake. No one could object to the removal of a leaf. It cost nothing and would remind her of all she had seen at Osborne House as well as if she had bought a snuff box or a letter opener from the gift shop. She hurried to catch up with Judy.

Judy paused where the path bent sharply to cross a little bridge. The sound of voices came from the other side—loud voices—but no one was visible for the trees.

"I tell yer, he's on to us! He's twigged!" A booming bass, stumbling to express the feelings of an inarticulate man.

"Nonsense, Grunt... you've just got the wind up... He's never had a line to me; you know I keep clean."

This voice was female, self-assured, and recognizable. Judy grabbed Margaret's arm and hissed, "Goldy Greening!" Stock still, scarcely breathing, they listened without shame. This was simply too interesting to be ignored.

Chapter 6
Mrs. Hark: Remedies

The Quists jogged up the path, calling "Does this go back to the bus?" and "Hi there! We've been all the way down to the beach!"

Judy Hark turned to Margaret Millet, whose face mirrored her own dismay. The conversation on the other side of the bridge stopped in mid-sentence, and heavy steps moved rapidly away. How exasperating! Then Judy's social sense came to her aid, and she faced the newcomers with a smile.

"We hope so. If not, we can get lost together. How was the beach?"

"Beautiful! But we hurried like anything to get back. It must be almost time to leave?" Vicky scarcely shortened her stride to pound across the little bridge.

The others followed, and at the car park, Judy caught a glimpse of Goldy Greening's billowing skirts disappearing into the bus. Davis followed. Yes! It had been Goldy telling "Grunt" Davis that she hadn't been "twigged" because she kept clean. But what could it mean? She must ask Margaret—but not in front of the Vics. She'd rather not admit to eavesdropping.

The white yachts of Yarmouth harbor skimmed turquoise waters sparkling with sun pennies. This ferry made a shorter crossing, and soon the great coach bowled along through green countryside. Sybil told her charges to watch for wild ponies as they entered the New Forest, and two ponies obligingly appeared, trotting along behind a fence at the edge of the road. They ran after the bus for a little way, then tossed their shaggy manes and turned aside.

"What pretty ponies," Judy said, "but where is the Forest? This is only woods and pastures." Judy, like Margaret, had grown up in the Pacific Northwest and expected a forest to be forested—to have large trees growing close together over a floor of moss and ferns.

Sybil gave them the history of this 90,000 acre tract of land, scarcely "new" as William the Conqueror had set it off to provide a Royal hunting ground. "To form the New Forest, families were evicted from more than thirty villages and forbidden to return," Sybil told them. "Under the law, a poacher could be blinded for killing the King's deer. Later, twelfth century historians wrote that the vengeance of God was visited upon William for these acts, when two of his sons and a grandson met their deaths in the New Forest."

Forest or woods, the place was beautifully natural, and the drive through grove, meadow, copse, and spinney—all words Judy found more appropriate than forest—a scenic delight.

They stopped for lunch at a wayside inn where roses nodded on the walls of a sunny courtyard.

"How good the sun feels. I'm glad we can sit outside," Margaret said, as they claimed a small white table and draped their wraps over the rustic chairs.

"Yes, and just the two of us. They seem kind of jammed together in there." Judy looked through the open French doors of the dining room, where half the tour group sat at a long trestle table, surrounded by running waitresses.

The Quists chose a spot in the courtyard and drew their chairs together, touching shoulders over a single menu. The tan man took the table just behind them. Freddie Factor followed him, and to Judy's surprise, Budge didn't seem to mind. Perhaps he was getting used to the brash New Yorker.

"It never fails," Freddie complained in his penetrating nasal tones, "traveling does it to me every time. I should have remembered and brought a laxative, but I left in such a hurry... wonder where I can find a drugstore in this—place?"

Budge said, "It's the restaurant food—lots of fat and no roughage. I carry something with me, if you'd like to try it." He pulled his satchel from under the chair, unzipped it, and fished inside.

"Airline food. That's what started it. Whatcha got, there? I'll take anything that'll do the job."

Judy found it hard to concentrate on the menu due to her distaste for Freddie and a strong desire not to hear about his bodily functions.

Budge held up a small box with a white label.

"Poison! Hey, I'm not taking any poison!" Freddie's voice rose even louder.

"Oh, dear. And it seemed so peaceful out here," Margaret muttered.

Budge said, "Well, they are poisonous if you take too many. That's why I labeled the box. It's a natural remedy I got in Barbados, called 'purge nuts.'" He opened the box and showed Freddie its contents. "You just use a tiny bit—best laxative in the world. And it tastes good—sort of like vanilla cream cookies. Here, I'll wrap some in a piece of napkin. Don't use it until tonight; it works pretty fast." He dropped the box in the pocket of his jacket.

Freddie expressed doubts and a continuing wish to find a drugstore, but he took the folded paper and stuck it in his wallet. The other lunchers turned away, and Sybil Darington, who had paused behind Freddie's chair, moved on, nodding to Goldy Greening and the Arvins on her way to a corner table.

Over a roast beef sandwich on fresh baked bread, Judy muttered, "I'm not going to let him spoil the trip for me, but that Freddie is too much. I still think he looks like a cheap crook."

"Do you think he might be the one who's "twigged?" Margaret asked.

"What does that mean, Margaret? Why does Goldy 'keep clean?' I don't get it."

"Yes, it was Goldy—and Davis—what did she call him?"

"Grunt! And it fits, you know?"

"The best translation I can give you," Margaret said, "is that Davis thinks someone has recognized them, and Goldy said no, this someone has never had reason to connect her with whatever it is they're talking about. What do you suppose is going on, anyway?"

"I do wish the Vics hadn't come bounding up just then! We might have found out."

"Oh, Judy, it doesn't concern us, surely. Let's just enjoy our trip and not worry about other people's problems. We promised Willy we'd stay out of trouble, remember?"

"Yes, you're right. It's my vivid imagination. But when you see people like Freddie—and Goldy Greening—well, I get nervous. Remember that theater trip we took, when the bus got held up?" Judy's forehead puckered in concern.

"I'll never forget it. What an adventure! And that nice young couple—I wonder if they ever got married?"

It was true that nobody had been hurt on that occasion, or even robbed, as it turned out. Judy relaxed and smiled. "We have had some times, haven't we?"

She sipped her tea and consented to thick, yellow cream over the pudding. Delicious! She could diet in California.

Goldy and Davis departed. After Jake Arvin videotaped the courtyard, he and Molly went inside, where he could be seen, camera to eye, recording the inn's interior.

In the far corner of the courtyard, Sybil Darington had been joined by a fair-haired young man who reached over the wall to coax one of the New Forest ponies with a piece of bread. Sybil's profile looked stormy. In a voice too low to hear, she seemed to be giving the young man a piece of her mind.

"Who's that, I wonder?" Judy indicated Sybil's companion.

"Oh!" Margaret inspected the young man's back with interest. "It looks like—wait 'til he turns around... Yes, he was in the pub, in Portsmouth."

"The pub in Portsmouth? You must be mistaken; it's someone who knows Sybil."

"It's the same man—remember, I asked you to look at him, because he seemed familiar—and now I see why. He looks like Sybil; I'll bet he's her brother..."

"I see a resemblance. But I don't remember him from the pub."

"Sitting with Goldy Greening, after everybody else left her table. Oh, it's the same man, all right."

"Suppose we could get an introduction?" Judy rose, a challenge in her eye, and picked up a carrot stick. She moved toward the wall and Margaret followed.

"How tame he is," Judy said as the pony drew back his upper lip and sniffed the bread in the young man's hand. "May I try? Here, little guy... oops, not the fingers, if you please..."

The pony snatched the carrot stick, shied and trotted off. Sybil brightened and said, pleasantly enough, "They are fun, aren't they?" She made no move to introduce the young man. Instead, she snatched up her bag and walked off, tossing her next remark over her shoulder; "We'd better get back to the coach. Broadlands this afternoon." The young man followed.

Margaret turned obediently to go, but Judy noticed a thicket near the wall vibrating in a curious way and paused. Malcolm emerged from it, bent over double, his eyes on the ground. With a pocket knife, he prodded the ground, then lifted something into a shoe box he carried.

"The bus won't leave without Malcolm," Judy observed.

"What's he doing?" Margaret came to the wall.

Malcolm worked his way toward them. The shoe-box held assorted greenery: leaves, dainty ferns, clumps of moss, and a plant with a tiny, white flower. He straightened, balanced the box on top of the wall, and vaulted lightly into the courtyard.

"Hello, ladies. Pickings are good today—care to see?" He held out the box for their inspection. "Specimens. I'm fond of plants. I've got books that tell what things are; I'll take these home and look 'em up, see?" Malcolm smiled with pleasure at his finds.

"How interesting! What's the little white flower, do you know?" Margaret asked.

"Not sure. I think it's one of the campions, Silene Alba, maybe. I need to check that, don't I? And this is a lichen, Cladonia Fimbriata." He pointed at a grayish clump of soft spikes shaped like golf tees, round and indented on the top.

"Some of the wild plants in the New Forest don't grow anywhere else. Even the tame things; there are apple trees so old that nobody knows the names of the apples anymore."

On the way back to the bus, Margaret said softly, "I do like a man to have unexpected sides to him, don't you?"

On the bus, Sybil Darington's bright head bent over her clipboard, checking off passengers along the aisle. As Malcolm eased the bus back onto the highway, a dilapidated convertible roared around them, making him brake suddenly and sound his horn. The rattletrap's fair-haired driver returned a brassy toot-toot of his own and swirled off in a cloud of dust, taking the direction from which the tour bus had come.

Sybil watched the roadster with brimming eyes and Judy simply did the appropriate thing; she reached across Margaret's lap and handed Sybil a clean tissue.

After mopping up, Sybil looked down at the sympathetic faces of the two ladies and said, "Bless you, Mrs. Hark." Then she bent back to her work.

Chapter 7
Mrs. Millet: Nothing But Trouble

Elaborate houses were not really Margaret Millet's "thing" but she had to admit that Broadlands, the home of Lord Louis Mountbatten, was impressive. The house sat on high ground above the River Teste. Sweeping lawns ran down to the deep, fast flowing stream and a flock of sheep, grazing on the other side, completed the pastoral scene.

Her poise recovered, Sybil informed them as the bus approached. "The topiary is yew, and the gardens were designed by Capability Brown," she said. "Broadlands came to Lord Mountbatten through his wife, Edwina Ashley, who grew up here. The estate farms two thousand acres, and was a favorite residence of the family until the terrible day in 1979, on the west coast of Ireland, when the silly Irish blew up Lord Mountbatten's boat. He, his grandson Nicholas, and the Dowager Lady Brabourne were killed, and other members of the family were seriously injured."

Sybil's voice was bitter as she said "the silly Irish," and Margaret felt sure a stronger adjective had been replaced.

"But pleasant things have happened at Broadlands," Sybil went on. "Prince Philip and Queen Elizabeth started their honeymoon here, as did Charles and Diana. The Mountbattens honeymooned here themselves. You'll see the Silver Ghost Rolls Royce that was Lady Edwina's wedding gift to her husband, displayed on the grounds."

"A Silver Ghost... I must take a picture of that for Tiny," Margaret said, thinking of her son-in-law's passion for old cars.

"Prince Philip is a Mountbatten, too," Judy said. "What relation is he to this one?"

"A nephew, I think. The name used to be Battenberg, but that's German, so they changed it. European royalty are all related, you know—Victoria had so many children, and they married all over the place. Philip came from Greece."

Judy had more questions, but Margaret had run out of answers, except for "Yes, Louis was the last Viceroy of India, just before England had to let it go; I remember that."

As at Osborne House, staff members led the tour through a portion of Broadlands carefully prepared for view with velvet ropes and carpeted aisles. Margaret shuffled along in line, listening to the oohs and aahs over tiaras and uniforms (of which the Mountbattens must have been extremely fond), but her interest was most aroused by the library. She could have spent days there. Instead of gloomy, leather-bound tomes, it was filled with biographies, stories of the sea, and all the best novels of modern times—exactly the books Margaret would possess if she had shelves to hold them and the funds to order each book as it came from the press.

"Look, still in dust jacket!" she exclaimed, pointing to a fine copy of *Love in a Cold Climate*—such a contrast to her own crumbling paperback. "I always wondered if Nancy Mitford based Lord and Lady Montdore on the Mountbattens, and here's the book in their own library!" She was so thrilled by this and other discoveries that she let the others go past her and had to be prized away from the shelves by a rear-guard staff member.

Back outside, the two ladies hiked the perimeter of Capability Brown's gardens (so shielded by the yew hedge as to be unviewable), and strolled toward stables and outbuildings some distance from the mansion. Margaret spotted the Rolls Royce she wanted to photograph just as Judy saw Sybil Darington, alone on a rustic bench.

"There it is. Let's see, how many do I have left?" Margaret checked her little point-and-shoot camera.

"I'll meet you back at the bus," Judy said.

Margaret watched Judy stride toward the bench and smiled—the odds were that Judy would soon know what had made Sybil Darington cry. Oh Willy, she sighed to herself, I can't help it, Willy. There's just no way to keep Judy from getting interested in other people's lives.

The Royal Plaza Hotel in Bournemouth, a structure of considerable magnificence, enjoyed breathtaking views of the sea and seemed superior to their hostelry in Portsmouth. They arrived earlier in the day as well, and Margaret ascribed both circumstances to the change in itinerary. It must have taken a good bit of juggling to find lodging for forty-eight tourists after the Southampton reservations fell through.

"Margaret! Heated towel bars—the towels are all warm!" Judy called from the bathroom, a glittering, white tiled chamber with a tub like a swimming pool.

Margaret stood by the window, admiring the view. Trees and brilliant flower beds bordered the seafront promenade, and a long pier extended into the water. "There's time for a walk before dinner. Care to join me? I want to buy some postcards and stamps. Wonder where the post office is?"

"I told Sybil I'd meet her in the bar. Do you mind? Get me some stamps, too, would you?"

"Okay. How many? And how is it with Sybil? You do plan to tell me, don't you? Is there anything we can do?"

"Of course I plan to tell you. After dinner."

"According to Malcolm, her brother 'blotted his copybook,' you know. Okay, after dinner..."

The gold braided doorman directed her to the post office, speaking slowly, as to a retarded child. It was only a five minute walk, but an open bookstore laid snares in Margaret's path. Wheeled shelves outside its portal were piled high with treasures. Only the thought of her crammed, overweight suitcases kept her in check. An ancient copy of *Raffles, the Amateur Cracksman* and a D. E. Stevenson paperback proved irresistible, and it might have been worse if the clerk hadn't trundled in the sidewalk shelves and said, "Closing time."

Telephone stalls lined one wall of the Bournemouth Post Office. As Margaret entered, she noticed the tan man, his back turned and a receiver clamped tightly to his ear. Curious, she paused behind him, looking at a poster on the wall.

"I tell you, I'm not in Southampton! No, the whole tour is in Bournemouth. Something about the regatta... Regatta! Boats... Yeah, that's right. Southampton was full up, so we're in Bournemouth. Well, I can't help it, how about Penzance? That should give you time..."

Budge sounded quite distressed. Margaret purchased her stamps, hoping the change in hotels hadn't seriously upset his plans.

Next door, a news stand displayed racks of postcards, and Margaret dawdled over her choices. From behind the racks, she saw Budge plodding toward the hotel, his satchel under one arm and his tan hat pulled down over his ears so only the round chin and downturned mouth were visible.

Margaret followed and saw him enter the hotel. Her eyes on Budge, she failed to notice the watcher coming along behind her, watching her watch Budge.

Margaret slowly advanced into the dim bar. Yes, Judy and Sybil had a booth in the far corner. Someone else, too—a dark head, just visible over the back of the booth. Malcolm? Good. Margaret moved closer, waiting for her eyes to adjust to the darkness. Three faces were lit by a candle flame, the perfection of Sybil's profile reflected in the brandy snifter she turned in her hands. Her soft voice murmured like an incantation.

Margaret said, "There you are. Is this a private seance? I didn't bring my crystal ball."

Sybil straightened and turned on her travel-guide smile. Judy said, "It's only Margaret. Sit by Malcolm, dear. Sybil is just telling us..."

"It's nothing—nothing at all." Sybil said. "Malcolm, why don't you get Mrs. Millet a drink?"

Malcolm smiled and slid out of the booth. "What would you like, Mrs. Millet?"

"I'd like a Guinness, if you please." Margaret rummaged in her purse for money.

Malcolm didn't wait, and Margaret felt guilty on two counts. Malcolm had other uses for his pay, and she apparently had barged into Sybil's unburdening. She tried to read Judy's expression, but could make nothing of it in the dim light. Well, it couldn't be helped. A glass of Guinness Stout would be a comfort.

Embarrassment made her babble. "I used to drink this in Santa Monica, at the old Mucky Duck," she said, when Malcolm brought her drink and slid in beside her. "The pub where all the English people in Los Angeles gathered. You could get wonderful fish and chips there, too. Almost broke my heart when they tore it down." She took a long swallow. "But I've interrupted you. Please, Sybil, do go on."

Sybil's bright-for-the-tourists face trembled around the edges.

Malcolm said, "I've talked to Mrs. Millet, love. She's all right, that one. Not apt to talk either, I'd say."

"Oh, no," Judy said. "Margaret's full of good sense. Maybe she can suggest something."

Margaret felt better after these testimonials and took another swig of her stout.

"It's Sybil's brother, Richard," Judy said.

Sybil thumped her brandy snifter on the table so hard it seemed likely to break, and said fiercely, "Yes, Mrs. Millet, it's my brother Richard! He's hopeless, I'm afraid. But I don't see what anybody can do about him—he's nothing but trouble, and always has been."

It took time and all Judy Hark's highly developed tact. Margaret watched her untangle the story, pulling first on one thread, then another, making helpful comments and listening intently as the tale unfolded.

The Darington family had suffered a disastrous crime three years before. Valuable gems were stolen. "All family things," Sybil said. "A diamond sunburst worn at the coronation of Queen Victoria. The Hortensia Pearls, even older and part of my great, great grandmother's dowry. Richard's wife, if ever there is one, should have worn them at her wedding. They even took the ruby that belonged to me, as the eldest daughter. And then, to cover up, they set fire to the house."

The fire did a great deal of damage, and worst of all, the insurance company refused to pay. The police claimed evidence of inside assistance to the burglars—by Richard, Sybil's brother. The insurance company claimed fraud. There was a trial, and while the Darington's high-priced lawyers managed to keep Richard out of jail, the verdict was "unproven."

"It's like Bleak House," Sybil said. "We're suing, the insurance people still won't part, and the lawyers will take all the money when, and if, they ever do."

Between the attorney's fees for Richard and the cost of rebuilding Darington Manor, the family's fortune had evaporated. Land was heavily mortgaged and lost. Then Sybil's mother died of cancer, and her father's health deteriorated. In an effort to help, Sybil had taken the job with Gateway World Tours. Richard still lived at home, "when he isn't racketing around the countryside, doing heaven only knows what."

During these revelations, they consumed more drinks, and decided to skip the hotel dining room in favor of meat pies where they were.

Sybil ate in an absent minded way, with the unimpaired appetite of youth. At last, she tucked a wayward lock behind her ear, spooned up the brown gravy from her dish and said, "And now, here comes dear Richard, saying he can fix everything if I'll just help him survive until he can pull it off! 'Pull what off?' I ask him. 'Never you mind,' he says. 'Trust me, and all will be well.' How can I trust him? What is he up to?"

The scene in the Portsmouth pub flashed into Margaret's mind—Richard Darington all cozy with Goldy Greening and her bodyguard, Grunt Davis.

"Was the... er... loot from your robbery ever recovered?" she asked.

"No! Not a single piece; how did you know?"

"You haven't seen anything familiar among Goldy Greening's diamonds?"

"Mrs. Millet—what do you mean? What are you saying?"

"Just that Goldy and your brother seem to be chums. I wondered if you knew. Goldy ignored him completely at lunch today, but unless Richard has a double, I saw them together at a pub in Portsmouth. They seemed very friendly indeed."

Sybil sat in stunned silence, and Margaret knew what she must be thinking. What could her brother possibly have in common with Goldy Greening, for whom "common" was the only word?

Malcolm patted Sybil's hand and said, "Now there's a bit of news? Something you might ask about? He couldn't be thinking of a rich marriage, I suppose—oh, no, not that."

Sybil's laugh was bitter. "Not likely. Richard's girls run young and penniless, as a rule. And self-sacrifice is not in his line. Oh God, I do hope he's not got himself into any more trouble. How did she get all those diamonds, does anyone know?"

"Married them, I expect," said Malcolm. "Classic story of Chorus Girl weds Nob? She must have been quite a bird, twenty years and fifty pounds ago."

It was late when they went upstairs, and Margaret longed for the comfy-looking hotel bed, but there were the postcards. She had promised a good many people to report what she found on this Magic Isle. Also, she wanted to get in touch with Bob Tyler in Manchester, if possible.

"I'm just going to say we're here. I'll give him a list of places where he can call, and tell him we have a free week at the end of the trip. If he wants to see us, he can let us know. Otherwise, I'd like to come back to Cornwall for that week—maybe Penzance, if we like it when the tour stops there."

Judy stuck her head out of the bathroom, a startling sight. Her face was covered with heavy white cream and her hairdo wrapped in a black turban. "That's where you might find your relations, isn't it? How exciting!"

"Well, they'd be pretty distant relations by now. But yes, that's where the Penfolds started out."

"We'll be in Plymouth tomorrow. Did any of them migrate on the Mayflower?"

"I don't think so. But they were in America before the Revolution. All good Tories except one—he joined up with Washington and the rest of them fled to Canada. Later they came back to Maine, and now they get into the D.A.R. on the strength of that one rebel."

"Doesn't the Western branch get into the D.A.R.?"

"They got over being Tories."

"Tell Bob I send greetings. I still like him, even if he did desert us in Texas."

"Okay. I still like him, too."

Chapter 8
Mrs. Hark: Devonshire Cream Tea

"I'm going to skip lunch, I think," Judy Hark helped herself to another egg, fresh and beautifully cooked. "They must use egg rings and steam to get these so nice. They can't be just fried." She really enjoyed English Breakfast Included.

She enjoyed Salisbury Cathedral, too, although it was under repair, and its beauty marred by scaffolding. The tallest spire in England, the high-flown arches and marble columns within, the tombs and effigies where Jake Arvin so assiduously focused his video camera; all were a wonder. Still, she knew what Margaret meant when she said, "It's marvelous, but what could it possibly have to do with Christ? He lived a simple, wandering life, teaching love and brotherhood."

Stonehenge was another matter.

The ancient ring of stones was fenced to protect it from the tourists. Judy stood close to the fence. "This place is awesome." Margaret, too, was profoundly impressed.

They circled the fence to view this prehistoric cathedral from all sides. Margaret stopped close to the Heel Stone and seemed rooted to the earth, unable to move. Then she gave a little shudder and strolled on. "I'd like to sit there for hours and hours. There's something here. Do you feel it? Even with all these people around—how strange. The only other place I've ever felt like this was in the Dunes south of Gambol Beach, where the Dunites lived. And I went there entirely alone."

Judy knew the place. During the Great Depression, it had been a haven for writers, artists, and advocates of the simple life. The Dunites camped out or lived in shacks, ate Pismo clams, and claimed that mystical powers rose out of the sand.

At the car park gift shop, Judy bought a booklet titled "The Prehistoric Temples of Stonehenge & Avebury." Much too soon, they were on the bus, rolling along toward their next stop. That was the trouble with a guided tour. Such a tight schedule, and only a small taste of each offering.

By microphone, Sybil said, "I know many of you wanted to stay longer at Stonehenge. It's a marvelous place, isn't it? Some people believe that lines of magnetic force meet there; you might like to read up on that theory. And there's a book about its astronomical significance, too.

"From carbon dating we know the site was in use almost 4800 years ago, about 2800 B.C., up to 1100 B.C., a period of some seventeen centuries. Early Christians thought it was an evil place built by the Devil, and there's a legend about how the Heel Stone got its name. A daring Christian Friar tackled the Devil while he was erecting the stones, the legend says. The Devil was furious and heaved this great, 35 ton stone at him, but the nimble Friar dodged, and it only struck his heel, doing him no harm. That's why it's called the Heel Stone, or the Friar's Heel. Aligned with other stones, the sun rises over the Heel Stone on Midsummer's Day, marking the summer solstice."

All the way to Exeter, Margaret seemed quiet and withdrawn. Judy couldn't remember when anything had penetrated her friend's exterior shell with such effect. Even when Jake Arvin came down the aisle to show them his map, Margaret took little interest in their route, or the fine "shots" Jake said he had taken of Salisbury Cathedral and its ancient predecessor.

To tell the truth, Judy didn't feel like talking either. Sybil Darington and her brother, Richard; what a sad story! Sybil's resentment and bitterness were natural enough. All her life, the family's best had gone to Richard; Eton, Oxford, the inheritance of Darington Manor and its lands. Even after the robbery and fire, something might have been salvaged if Mr. Darington had been willing to move into their farmhouse, keep the land, and let Richard face up to English justice with the aid of the family solicitor. Sybil had made that very clear.

But Judy felt sorry for Richard, too. What impossibly high expectations he faced, as a member of the Landed Gentry! In her world, a boy had only to be decent and hold down a job for people to say he turned out well, while Richard was expected to take care of a mansion full of treasures and a large farm, and make a "good marriage," to boot. Not to mention producing and rearing an heir. No wonder he cracked under the strain and did foolish things.

And now he had a scheme to recoup the family fortunes. What could it be? Some of the "noblesse oblige" must have stuck; he still wanted to be St. George and slay the dragon for his family.

In Exeter, Judy and Margaret did skip lunch to exchange traveler's checks for English money at a bank. Judy bought apples at a fruit stand, in case they got hungry later. It was good to walk around, and she climbed back into the bus with some reluctance. Due to the day's rotation, their seats were at the very back, and she felt woozy from the sway.

Freddie Factor didn't care for the bus's rear end, either. "Boy, sitting back here is worse than riding a camel," he said to the tan man.

Budge replied, "No, it's not. Did you ever ride a camel?" Budge had, and told Freddie all about it.

In Devonshire now, they rolled over Dartmoor; green fields between hedges and stone walls, then open moorland with gorse and blooming heather. The grim, grey buildings of Dartmoor Prison loomed in the distance.

Some time later, Malcolm pulled the bus over and Sybil said, "A view spot. You can see for miles from here, and the village of Widecombe-in-the-Moor lies just below. We stop there for a traditional Devonshire Cream Tea."

The passengers disembarked, stretched and took deep breaths of the fresh, heather-scented air—except the smokers, who inhaled their own atmosphere.

"Have you noticed that we always seem to stop for the view just when the smokers can't stand it any more?" Judy watched Molly Arvin drag on her cigarette.

"I think you're right," Margaret said. "Funny they never say so. It's always called a view spot or a photo opportunity."

They looked down at Widecombe, a tiny village tucked into a fold of the moor, surrounded by a checkerboard of richly green fields and dark hedgerows. A few minutes later, the bus descended a narrow, twisting road past small houses and shops, and rolled by the Roadside Cafe, where a teapot shaped sign announced, "HOMEMADE CAKES and SCONES."

The entire staff of the Roadside Cafe stood out in front to welcome them, flapping their orange aprons as the bus rolled in. The "tea" was ready, laid out on long tables; a meal of huge, fluffy, baking powder biscuits, strawberry jam, and bowls of Devonshire Cream. Waitresses brought fresh, hot tea.

While they ate, their host, in his orange apron, stood on a chair and educated them. The baking powder biscuits were "scones." Devonshire cream was made by slowly cooking rich cream over hot water until it evaporated to a thick, spreadable texture. Nothing was added. The result was simply intensified cream, and with strawberry jam, it turned a plain biscuit to ambrosia.

"Always thought scones were pastry sort of things," Judy said, deeply thankful she had skipped lunch.

"So did I. Another difference in language, I guess. Best biscuits I ever ate. They deserve to be called scones." Margaret spooned the thick cream onto another one.

After their feast, most of the tourists queued to purchase small cartons of the Devonshire Cream. The cashier, a pert, smiling teenager, assured them the cream would keep for several days without refrigeration. "That's why they cook it in the first place," she said.

Tony Budge pushed past the queue, jogging Judy's elbow just as she opened her coin purse. Several coins fell on the floor, but he didn't stop to help her find them. How rude, she thought, and said so to Margaret when they got outside.

"How rude! He could have helped me pick them up."

"Stingy, too," Margaret said. "He ate more cream than anybody, but he was too cheap to buy some." The Devonshire Cream Tea was one of the treats included in the tour package.

The bus climbed out of Widecombe on a lane barely one vehicle wide, hedgerow branches scraping both sides. Three quarters of the way to the top of the moor, they met a van and Malcolm had to back the huge coach down again, all the way to the bottom. From their rear seats, the ladies could see what a feat of skill it was, and they led the cheers when the van finally had room to squeeze by. "Malcolm is my hero!" Margaret cried, and Judy felt it was well said.

Safely back on the main road, Sybil beguiled the hours with tales of ancient days in Devon. "Plymouth means the Pilgrims to Americans, but to the English, it means Sir Francis Drake and the Spanish Armada. When Drake looted enormous treasure from Spanish ships, Philip of Spain demanded his head, but Elizabeth held a state banquet on Drake's ship and knighted him, instead.

"Eight years later, Philip's Armada sailed up the English Channel. Drake and Lord Howard were playing a game of bowls on a hilltop above Plymouth when they got word that the Armada was off the Lizard, only sixty miles away. This is the poem Henry Newbolt wrote about it:

"He was playing at Plymouth a rubber of bowls
When the great Armada came;
But he said, 'They must wait their turn, good souls,'
And he stooped and finished the game."

"Many people believe that Drake's Drum is heard when England is in peril. Newbolt wrote about that, too:

"Roving though his death fell, he went with heart at ease,
  And dreaming all the time of Plymouth Hoe.
'Take my drum to England, hang it by the shore,
  Strike it when your powder's running low;
If the Dons sight Devon, I'll quit the port o'Heaven,
  And drum them up the Channel as we drummed them
long ago.'"

Revived and heartened by the cream tea and Sybil's stories, Judy postponed her weariness. Margaret seemed more cheerful, too, and bubbled with joy when they passed a thatched cottage, with its high piled roof of straw.

In Plymouth, Judy was amused to note that the tour already dined by habit, the same people at table together. After a few faces became familiar, one clung to them rather than make the effort to find new ones.

The Quists hadn't changed for dinner and wore matching grey jerseys over white shirts. Jake Arvin brought his map and Freddie Factor shared Molly's ash tray.

"Wonder what happened to Budge?" Freddie said, as a platter of roast beef made the rounds. "Not like him to be late for dinner."

"Maybe he's trying to get his mail," Margaret said.

"Maybe he's found a livelier place to eat." Freddie waved a hand at the formal dining room. "This place could use a juke box. As much fun as a high-tone funeral parlor."

Judy smiled, remembering Margaret's comment in Widecombe. "I think he'll be along. Dinner is included in the tour."

She was right. The tan man slipped into his chair unobtrusively. He wasn't there and then he was, eating his dinner from a plate no one had seen him fill.

The waiters cleared the main course and brought pound cake and hard sauce. Jake flourished his map. "It's not far to

Penzance; short ride tomorrow. Cornwall is just across this bay. Oh, it's not a bay. It's Plymouth Sound." He pointed out the name on his map.

"Cornwall," Margaret sighed. "Cornwall at last. Tristan and Isolde..."

She hated to admit it, but Judy Hark was thoroughly done in, exhausted, used up. As they trudged up two flights of stairs to their room, she proposed an early night.

Tired as she was, after she got to bed her mind refused to sleep. Instead, it brought up one personality after another for her consideration.

Freddie Factor might be more than an annoyance, she thought. She didn't like the way his eyes roamed, never still, always moving from one person to another. And Goldy Greening hadn't shown up at dinner. In the dark ebb of the night, Goldy's absence seemed fraught with meaning. That bodyguard of hers; another unsavory type. And Richard Darington—would he turn up again? What would happen in Penzance?

Chapter 9
Mrs. Millet: Watch the Wall, My Darling

In her journal, Margaret Millet wrote "I looked in the Plymouth telephone book, and there were no Penfolds listed." She was jarred and disturbed by the absence of Penfolds in Plymouth. For the first time, it occurred to her that the English branch of the family might have died out entirely. Had they all emigrated to America? Well, she would keep looking. Maybe they just didn't care for Plymouth.

She wrote, "More and more, I feel that England and its history belong to me, as much as they belong to the English. Anything that happened before 1750 is as much mine as theirs. It's just that my ancestors went to America and theirs stayed home."

The tour spent the morning of "Day Four" in Plymouth. "A free morning to relax and explore this historic city, enjoy a walk across the Hoe, shop in the Barbican or take an optional cruise around Plymouth Sound to see the great naval warships," said the trip brochure.

At the hotel desk, the ladies learned that Plymouth Hoe was a bluff overlooking the harbor, and "Hoe" simply meant "high place."

"Let's shop," Margaret said. "We haven't had much time for it, so far on this trip."

They were directed to The Barbican, a shopping area built along ancient fortifications. On the way, they passed the Plymouth Steps, the stone landing where the Mayflower had taken on her passengers. Island House, nearby, had a tall sign board on its wall listing the names of the Mayflower passengers.

"No Penfolds," Margaret said. "I didn't think so. No religious fanatics in the family, even then."

The shops sold trinkets dear to a tourist's heart; some were of local craftsmanship. Margaret bought two silver pins in Celtic designs; one for her daughter and the other, because she couldn't resist it, for herself.

The bus entered Cornwall on a high bridge over the Tamar River, giving them a magnificent view down Plymouth Sound. To Margaret it felt like vaulting the waterway on fantastic stilts, instead of rolling across a bridge. Sybil added to the magic by chanting the rule for Cornish surnames, "By Tre, Pol, and Pen, know ye Cornish men," and she cited Squire Trelawney, in *Treasure Island* as a classic example. The Penfolds, too, Margaret thought.

They stopped for lunch in Looe, a fishing village and former smuggler's port, where stout little houses clung to steep hills around a harbor full of boats.

Sybil said, "The south coast of England is pocked with rocky coves and beaches. In the old days, goods from France and Holland were landed on dark, foggy nights, to avoid the King's tax collectors. This is Kipling's poem about the smugglers, from Puck of Pook's Hill:

"If you wake at midnight and hear a horse's feet,
Don't go drawing back the blind, or looking in the street,
Them that asks no questions isn't told a lie.
Watch the wall, my darling, while the Gentlemen go by!
Five and twenty ponies,
Trotting through the dark—
Brandy for the Parson,
'Baccy for the Clerk;
Laces for a lady; letters for a spy,
And watch the wall, my darling, while the Gentlemen go by!"

Margaret and Judy walked along the waterfront to a pub where they watched the white swans of Looe Harbor and consumed crab sandwiches and ale.

None of the other tourists had come this far, so they eyed the local pub-goers. A man at the next table, the picture of John Bull, put away his pints in rapid succession. As he carried the third mug from the bar, he nearly sloshed ale on Judy and stopped to apologize.

"Sorry! Don't have much time, y'know—wife's shopping, she'll be back soon."

Judy grinned. "It's okay, you missed me. Won't your wife join you when she comes?"

"Gar she'd like to, but it's not safe! She's drivin' the car—werry strict they are about drink while driving." The man shook his head sorrowfully and drank, his red face aglow. It was evidently a sore subject, and after they chatted, the man asking questions about America and the ladies about Cornwall, he reverted to it.

"Werry strict... those lads can stop you any time, can't they? Make you blow into their machine, and hike you off to the lock-up! Werry strict."

John Bull had a snootful by the time the ladies started back to the bus. "Hope he won't be in too much trouble with his wife," Margaret remarked. "Wonder if she regulates her shopping time to his ale capacity?"

"If so, she should have cut it short today," Judy said.

From Looe, the tour took a scenic route through Truro and St. Ives to the westernmost bit of England. A wonderful day for smuggling at Land's End; fog thick enough to swim in, and visibility down to ten feet or less in any direction—not a good day for the fabled Atlantic view.

Margaret spotted Jake Arvin, minus his video camera for once, hunched beneath the "Land's End" sign post at the edge of the cliff. White arrows on the post read "Wolf Rock Lighthouse 8," "Scilly Isles 28," and "John O'Groats 874." Jake's fists were jammed in the pockets of his black windbreaker, and he gazed into the white fog as though he had x-ray vision. He'll make an interesting silhouette against the fog, Margaret thought, as she snapped a picture.

Approaching Penzance, they left fog behind. Malcolm turned off the main highway and made them a present of Mount's Bay. From Newlyn Harbor to St. Michael's Mount, the sun sparkled on water of deepest blue. The tide was out, exposing the rocky spine that connected St. Michael's Mount to the mainland; part of an ancient land bridge to Europe, Sybil told them.

The Monarch in Penzance was the most elegant hostelry of the tour so far, which only made things more difficult for Sybil, because the Monarch had overbooked. Some of the tour members would have to be housed in a lesser establishment.

To be fair, no one could check in until this problem was solved. The tour group milled about, grumbling at the delay, and Goldy Greening was particularly displeased.

"We booked months ago! Here, now—let's have our rooms, awr eye?" She leaned on the reception counter, flashing her diamonds, while Grunt Davis glowered behind her. The hotel manager flapped and fluttered, finally letting her sign a registration card, but withholding the room key.

"Or I? What does she mean? Why should she be special?" Judy muttered.

"Or I—oh, she meant 'all right.' You have to listen in British," Margaret said.

Sybil had disappeared behind the counter, and after a frustrating quarter-hour, she returned. "We've found accommodations at the Pettit, a very exclusive private hotel just a few blocks away. They have two single rooms and one double. The Monarch's limo will take you over, bring you back for dinner, and pick you up in the morning. We and the Monarch sincerely regret the inconvenience, and we're sure those who go to the

Pettit will find it very comfortable."

The two single rooms meant Tony Budge and Freddie Factor, who grumbled but agreed. When no volunteers came forward for the double, Sybil approached Margaret and Judy. They had befriended her, and she asked their help.

"I'm too tired to care where I sleep, as long as I can do it soon," Judy declared. "I didn't sleep a wink last night—well, hardly a wink. Come on, Margaret, let's make sure they find our suitcases, and go along."

In the limo, Freddie laughed and told a bawdy joke about a salesman who got into the wrong hotel room. The limo driver's neck stiffened above his uniform collar, and Margaret winced. She could hear him thinking "Americans!"

"Where's the post office?" Budge pulled on the back of Margaret's seat and called to the driver. "Will I be able to walk to the post office from this Pettit Hotel?"

"Yes sir," the driver said. "I'll show you." He turned a corner and stopped in the middle of the block. "You ladies don't mind?"

Here was the post office. The driver hopped out and opened Budge's door with exaggerated courtesy. Budge jerked in surprise, then recovered his poise and got out. Halfway across the sidewalk he stopped short, started to turn, and then went on. His tan satchel lay on the seat of the limo, and Margaret wondered if he had suddenly noticed his hands were empty. She had often experienced the same jolt from leaving her purse behind.

"I really am exhausted," Judy said. "I don't think I can face getting dressed and going back for dinner." The corners of her mouth drooped in a most unusual way.

Alarmed, Margaret said, "Maybe we can get something at the Pettit. We'll eat in the room, and get a good rest." If Judy was losing her steam, Margaret would be happy to forgo her dinner. It was unheard of—she felt fine, and Judy could normally dance her under the table, any night of the week.

"Don't be nice to me," Judy said. "The Monarch looks like a marvelous place—why should you miss your dinner?"

"I don't mind, really."

"Nonsense. I'll stay in tonight, and you go out. You don't have to nursemaid me."

How cranky she sounded. Maybe she needed an evening alone—twenty-four hours a day was a lot of togetherness, after all. "Well, if you're sure. I would like to see more of Penzance."

Tony Budge emerged from the post office carrying a packet the size of a thinnish brick, plastered with English stamps. The driver smartly opened the limo door. Budge entered, and quickly stowed the packet away in his satchel. He held the bag on his lap for the rest of the drive, and gave the merest nod when Margaret said, "Did you get what you expected? How nice."

What could it be? Why was he so secretive? He had wanted to pick it up later, when he was alone, that was obvious. When the limo driver came straight to the post office, he didn't like it a bit—but didn't want to make a fuss. How odd.

The limo took three diners back to the Monarch Hotel, and Margaret joined her fellow travelers in the lounge, to wait for the dinner gong. They had all dressed, bow ties and cocktail gowns; she should have listened to Judy and worn something more glamorous than her all purpose navy pants-suit.

The Australian school teachers were sharing a London Times. As she approached them to ask for news of the world, Malcolm came up behind her and tapped her shoulder.

"Evening, Mrs. M. All alone? Where's your friend?"

Margaret explained. "But I'm not tired. After dinner, I want to see the town and walk on the Esplanade."

"Why wait 'til after dinner? The Smuggler's Inn has the best steak and kidney pie in Cornwall. Lots more fun than sticking around with this lot." He had changed his uniform for blue jeans and a jersey pullover, and eyed the overdressed tourists with a mixture of amusement and scorn.

"That's the best offer I've had all day. But only if you let me pay my share! I can afford it, really. I'm temporarily rich."

Malcolm gave her Sybil's seat in the front of the bus, and drove all around Penzance, so she could see the sights before dark. They went up Morrab Road past Penlee Park, where palm trees could be seen over the walls.

"It's a sub tropical garden, you see. Penzance faces south and has mild winters because of the warm ocean currents hereabouts," Malcolm said, and Margaret remembered his botanical interests.

She had never had so much fun in a bus; Malcolm tooled it around the town like a taxi. She loved the tall row houses on Upper High Street, white and blue and pink, with their chimney stacks and steep roofs. She looked down Causeway Head, still rife with shoppers, and laughed at the name "Market Jew Street." An open-air market flourished there once a week, Malcolm told her.

He finally parked the coach in a car park below the railroad station, and they proceeded on foot.

Approaching The Smuggler's Inn, they could see the "smuggler," a dark dummy peering over the ridge of the Inn's hip roof. The outer walls were white plaster in horizontal ridges, and they descended to the cellar by a steep, dark stair to a private booth, dimly lit by candles.

The Smuggler's steak and kidney pie was delicious, as Malcolm had promised. Margaret had never tasted anything quite like it. She said so, and Malcolm beamed with pleasure.

"You're temporarily rich then, Mrs. Millet. Tell me."

So she did. She told him the whole story; how she'd always wanted to visit England and never expected to, and how the mortgage money had come in all at once and Judy had agreed to come along. She tried to say how much the trip meant to her, but got a great lump in her throat and had to stop and drink some ale, instead.

What a lovely experience! Malcolm was wonderful. His

thick dark hair, his sturdy breadth of shoulder, and above all, his kindness to an old woman... what a shame for Judy to miss this remarkable evening!

After dinner they strolled along the Esplanade under an autumn moon that dappled the sea. Malcolm pointed out the Sailor's Mission, a two-story building of red brick with a crenelated tower.

"How well you know the town," Margaret said.

"Should do. Me mum was born here."

"But I thought she lived in Manchester?"

"Aye. She'd love to come back."

Even this lovely evening had to end. They turned away from the sea and climbed a steep, narrow side street leading back to the Pettit Hotel.

Malcolm paused on the sidewalk, scrutinizing a shabby convertible parked at the curb. "Here now. Look at that."

Mrs. Millet looked. Yes, she had seen the car before, in the New Forest. The jalopy Richard Darington drove, the day he made Sybil cry.

Chapter 10
Life of a Courier

Don't know when I've been so tired, Judy Hark thought, trudging up the richly carved mahogany staircase behind Mrs. Millet. She scarcely registered the grace and comfort of the beautiful old Pettit Hotel, except to note that it had no elevator. At least they were on the second floor. Budge and Freddie had to climb another flight, to the third.

She sank into the bed pillows and muttered proper responses until Margaret had dressed and gone, then picked up the telephone and asked for hot tea and something to go with it. "I don't really care what. I'm too tired to eat a meal. Bread and butter will be fine."

The tea was slow in coming, but worth the wait. A silver service on a huge tray, with buns, a small cake, fresh butter molded to the shape of a fat hen, and berry jam.

"Yes, put it there." Judy indicated the bedside table and gave the waiter one of the thick one-pound coins she had acquired in change, while shopping.

The waiter beamed, "Thank you, Madam!" and made a rapid and graceful exit. Apparently, a pound was a good tip.

Judy drank her first cup of tea, gaining the strength to butter a bun and spread it with jam. My, she was hungry after all! She ate everything except the last bit of cake (left for Miss Manners) and set the devastated tray out in the hall.

Now for a rest, followed by a shower and shampoo. She

washed out her undies and hung up a tailored linen dress for the next day. Something to read—she would try Margaret's battered copy of *Raffles, The Amateur Cracksman.* It looked small and light, just right for relaxation. How silly she'd been the night before, fretting and worrying about people she would never meet again. Her concern for Sybil had got out of proportion because she was over-tired, that's all. She just needed a quiet evening to herself.

Almost to herself. The only interruption was the delivery of mail from the Monarch; a fat envelope for Margaret from her daughter in Gambol Beach. Judy accepted it through the letter slot without opening the door and left it, prominently displayed, on the dresser. The rest of the evening went as planned.

Tony Budge enjoyed the splendors of the Monarch Hotel and the fine gourmet dinner served there. He would never have eaten such a meal if it had not come with the tour; when he had to pay, he settled for simpler pleasures. He said something to this effect to his tablemates, and then issued an invitation.

"Don't suppose there'll be any night life 'til nine o'clock or so, but if anyone would care to hit the pubs with me, I'll start out from the Pettit about then. I'm in room 12."

The Monarch offered an orchestra and dancing after nine, and Freddie, who was actually wearing a tie, said he planned to "whirl a few skirts." The Arvins and the Quists had also dressed with dancing in mind. Goldy grinned and waved "Attaboy" from the next table, and Sybil Darington, seated with a New Zealand couple, smiled at the conviviality of the usually antisocial Budge.

At the Pettit, Budge got his key from the desk clerk, went upstairs, wrote a postcard to his mother, and washed his underwear, hanging three pairs of boxer shorts over the shower pole. (In contrast to his tan exterior, the shorts blazed with stripes and polka dots.) He had just completed this task when the watcher knocked.

Budge opened the door. "Hel—lo. So it's you. What's the word?"

"Emerald."

"Right. The package is right here in my satchel. I haven't opened it yet, but your lot is supposed to be there."

"Good, I'm anxious to see them. I've brought the money."

"Let's see it, friend."

The watcher's face tensed, then smoothed into a knowing smile. "As soon as I see the stones. But look, you've told the world you're out for some fun tonight. Let's go out and have it—with plenty of witnesses. Here, I brought you something."

"Hey, Devonshire Cream! That stuff is really good."

"There's plenty left. Brought a couple of scones, too. It should be easy to handle our drinks with that in our stomachs. Here's a spoon—go ahead, pile it on."

At the inn in the New Forest, the watcher had deftly extracted Budge's box of Barbados purge nuts from his jacket pocket. Budge didn't miss it, didn't realize he hadn't dropped the box back in his satchel. Earlier that evening, using a soap dish and a hairbrush handle, the poisonous nuts had been mashed very fine and mixed thoroughly with the Devonshire Cream. Their pleasant taste may even have enhanced the flavor of the cream-piled scone. The watcher had only to talk—on topics of mutual interest, such as precious gems—until the poison took effect.

"What will you tell your boss about the stones?"

"That they weren't in the packet when it came." Budge winked. "That happens sometimes. The boys who do the lifting don't always get what they're sent for."

"But these are the cream of the collection. If I told you what they're really worth..."

"Cream, that's good." Budge chuckled and licked up some of the Devonshire Cream as it oozed off the scone. "Yummy, this is the cream."

"But my stones..."

"I know. Two carved emeralds the size of peach pits, from the treasure of some old Pope—museum stuff. Well it's my word against theirs. Just you see that those stones never turn up again. That's the agreement, and that's why I can give you a good price. Bury them, do what you like, but they never see the world again—not 'til I'm dead and gone. What d'ya want them for, anyhow? Shame to cut them up, but you'd have to, to sell them."

The watcher's eyes gleamed. "Money, that's all you think of. My collector wants the stones and he'll pay. Do you plan to carry the cash on you?"

"Not on your life. I'll wire it to my Swiss bank. All the years I've carried, I've never been caught, 'cause I've never spent the money. Saved it all, in Switzerland. I plan to retire and buy my own island one of these days."

Rarely, almost never, did Budge have a chance to discuss his real life's work—transporting stolen goods. He was a professional. He knew how; the techniques, the ways to go unchallenged, the details of innocence and anonymity. Like any successful careerist, he took pride in his skills. He had studied, practiced, paid his dues.

Budge happily took advantage of his safe audience to puff his talents. "Budge delivers," he said. "That's my motto. I've carried three times a year for the last seventeen years—millions of dollars worth. Only once—and that could have happened to anybody, see—three years ago, when the IRA was doing their bombs, the English cops searched everything. But I tumbled to it and stashed the goods. Plan to pick them up soon. You'd be surprised if you knew where..."

Yes, Budge thought. I could give you some real surprises. I'll pick up those jewels tonight. That was a close squeak, though. Took ten years off my life when I spotted that copper searching the luggage.

He went on to boast of the ease and dispatch with which he transported stolen valuables. Best audience he'd ever had.

"I've got the perfect cover," he said. "I live at home and take care of my mother. I go to work at the post office every day. I never travel alone; always with a tour. My life is an open book."

Budge smirked with self-satisfaction until the first pains gripped his abdomen. He caught his breath. Pain turned to agony, and he doubled over, gasping.

"You're ill, man! I'll fetch a doctor—"

The killer helped Budge to the bed, placed the little box marked POISON on the bedside table and retreated to a corner, out of Budge's view. Budge couldn't yell because he couldn't breathe. His legs contorted in painful cramps, his stomach tried to purge itself in both directions. He struggled off the bed, saw the box, and realized what had been done to him as he collapsed on the Persian carpet.

The killer knelt beside him and whispered hoarsely, "Every job a success but one. Where are they stashed, Budge? Tell me. I'll fetch them for you. Where, Budge? Where?"

Budge's eyes rolled up and his back arched with effort. He said a few garbled words. Then he died, with the poison box clenched tightly in his hand. It was 9:44 P.M., Penzance time.

The killer opened the tan satchel and tore into the parcel that had come to Penzance by the Royal Mail. There they were. The emeralds made pools of green fire in the light of the bedside lamp. In this hard material, the ancient, exquisite carvings were as clear as when they left the artist's hand, a head of Hercules on one stone, the flowing robes of Pallas Athene on the other. The lesser gems were a treasure in themselves, unmounted rubies and diamonds, each with a history of its own. After a brief, feverish inspection, the gems were fitted into a receptacle prepared for that purpose.

The killer had been careful about fingerprints, and now wiped the doorknob and other surfaces that might have been touched.

Budge's cameras and lenses were dumped on the bed, and the satchel used to carry the loot away, as well as the package wrappings and all evidence of food. After it served this purpose, the satchel would be disposed of... in a useful way.

Chapter 11
Mrs. Hark: Where is The Tan Man?

"So, how are things at home?" Judy asked over breakfast at the Monarch.

On this sparkling seaside morning the ladies had enjoyed a brisk walk down the stone paved Penzance streets from the Pettit Hotel; a little exercise before another day on the bus. On Day Five, the tour crossed to the north coast Of Cornwall, stopping in Tintagel, "birthplace of King Arthur; time to explore his ruined castle before we continue to Exmoor National Park and Lynton in the heart of Lorna Doone country." Or so said the trip brochure.

Margaret pulled her daughter's letter out of her purse. "I haven't opened it yet. Let's see."

Judy could not have left a letter unopened. Perhaps Margaret hadn't noticed it last night—and things had been rather a rush this morning.

"Well, for goodness sake!" Margaret picked up a bright green picture postcard that had dropped out of the letter. "From Bob Tyler—sent to Gambol Beach! Didn't he get my letter about coming to England?" She turned the card in her hand, examined both sides, and passed it over to Judy. The card pictured a Kiwi bird in the bush environment of New Zealand, all trees and moss and huge green ferns.

Judy handed it back. "Well, read it, Margaret, and see what he says."

Margaret was reading Laura's letter. "'This card came right after you left. Hope it gets to you, as I know you wanted to visit Bob in England, and it looks like he's not there. So sorry, Mom. Hope it won't spoil your trip...' Well, it won't spoil my trip, nothing could do that." She read on. Things were fine in Gambol Beach. Laura had talked to Willy, and he was fine, too.

Then Margaret picked up the postcard. "Let's see what he's got to say for himself. If possible. His handwriting! 'Hi there good buddy hope all is'—what's that, can you tell?"

Between them, like code-breakers, they deciphered the crowded hieroglyphics on the card; " ...hope all is good with you. Happy Christmas and all the best for next year. Currently on World Tour. Itinery (sic) UK, Ireland, France, Hawaii (not placed in Hula contest), N.Z., Bali, Japan, Singapore, Thailand, S. Africa, UK next June. Please keep in touch. Love, Bob XX."

"Well, how do you like that!" Judy exclaimed. "Next June! How do you suppose he's traveling for it to take so long?"

"Sounds like the slow boat to China," Margaret said. "Maybe a freighter; some of them take passengers."

"Well, he picked a great time to see the world. When did you write to him about our trip? Did he know we were coming before he left?"

Margaret said she had no idea when Bob left home, but looked guilty and finally admitted, "Maybe not. I didn't write until just before we started—didn't want to jinx the trip. He probably knows now, though. I expect his mail is forwarded to him, like it was on his trip to the U.S."

Judy was not fooled. Her friend had taken the disappointment well, but she could tell it hurt. Margaret prodded her English breakfast with a fork, but most of it stayed on her plate.

Sybil checked off the passengers as they climbed into the bus, laughing and chattering, ready for another day's adventure. She led the ceremonial chant, "Good Morning, Malcolm!" and asked if they had remembered to rotate their seats.

Margaret turned to Freddie Factor and asked, "Where's Mr. Budge?"

Freddie shrugged. "Beats me—I had the limo to myself this morning—thought he might be with you."

"Goodness, I hope he gets here!"

Just then Sybil noticed the empty seat and announced "We have a missing passenger." She looked at Freddie and added, "It's Mr. Budge, isn't it? Has anyone seen him?"

Heads shook, no one spoke. Sybil consulted Malcolm and said, "Our schedule is tight today, and it's time to start, so we'll go to the other hotel and pick him up there. Please watch out the windows and let me know if you see him on the street."

The bus moved away from the curb. Sybil stashed her clipboard and swayed down the aisle. "Mr. Factor? I wonder if you would go into the Pettit to ask about Mr. Budge?"

Freddie said firmly, "I'd rather not."

This rude response—from a man—must have been a new experience for Sybil. She straightened, glanced around to see who had heard the exchange, and met the concerned faces of Mrs. Millet and Mrs. Hark. They were happy to help.

"I wonder if he checked out," Margaret said. "Let's ask at the desk."

Budge had not checked out, and his passport, a forlorn leftover, still lay on the counter.

"He must have overslept!" Judy said. "Oh, dear, what if he's still asleep?"

The clerk suggested they go to the room, number 12 on the second floor, and "knock him up," an expression that made the ladies chortle in delight.

"Remember the second floor is really the third floor," Margaret started up the stairs. "They call the second floor the first floor, you know, and the first floor the ground floor. Confusing, isn't it?"

"Yes! I hope the bus will wait for him—it throws everything

out—he's going to upset everybody!"

With these prophetic words, Judy walked down the wide, carpeted hallway and knocked sharply on the door of number 12.

No reply. The ladies exchanged nervous glances, and Judy knocked again.

No reply.

"What if he's sick? What if he's had a heart attack?" Margaret fretted. "Let's go back and tell Sybil. Somebody should check in there!"

The hotel housekeeper came into view, pushing a cart of cleaning supplies, and the sight of her sturdy, aproned figure was a great relief. When told the situation, she banged on the door (loud enough to raise the dead, Judy thought), then turned her key in the lock and said, "Help yourself, ladies." She pushed her cart on down the hall.

Margaret hesitated and stepped back, unwilling to enter the bedroom of a man she scarcely knew. Judy squared her shoulders and moved up to the door, opened it about six inches, and called, "Hoo hoo! Mr. Budge!"

She opened the door wider and saw the side of the bed, the covers pulled half off and dragged to the floor. She caught a nasty, recognizable smell of vomit and feces.

The twisted form of Tony Budge lay on the carpet, his white shirt horribly soiled, his face blank and staring, empty of life. No amount of knocking would ever waken him again.

In slow motion, Judy pulled the door shut and turned, leaning her back against the wall. Her knees turned to custard and she slid gently to the floor.

"Don't go in there, Margaret. The man is dead."

Chapter 12
Mrs. Millet: Tour Interrupted

Margaret Millet had no desire to open the door on something that made Judy Hark collapse in that fashion. "Don't try to get up, Judy. Put your head between your knees." She knelt and chafed Judy's limp wrists.

"Sakes! She has had a turn, now, hasn't she?" The housekeeper. "Shall I go for salts?"

"Go down and send for a doctor, please. The man in number 12 is very sick. Oh, and tell our tour guide, would you? The bus is right outside. I'll stay with my friend."

The woman scuttled down the hall.

The hotel manager came first, followed by the broad, comforting figure of Malcolm, bounding up the stairs two at a time. Judy recovered enough to say, "You can't help him, he's gone," and a hasty peek into the room convinced the manager she was right.

"Here, let's not leave these ladies in the hall," Malcolm said.

"Of course, of course." The manager brushed imaginary specks off his dark suit and shot his shirt cuffs. He had busy hands, small and white, with a gold signet ring on one finger. "Come down to the lounge, Ladies, while we see what's to do."

Malcolm helped Judy to her feet, the manager took her other arm, and together they eased toward the main staircase. Margaret started to follow, then noticed a door ajar at the end of the hallway; had the housekeeper returned by the service stairs?

"Someone should stay here until the doctor comes," she said, and turned back. Judy gave her a reproachful glance, and Margaret made a face, trying to indicate that she had a good reason.

She was right; the housekeeper was dying to get into Budge's room. "Do you think we should have a look see? Wot's 'is trouble, then? Can we do sumpfing?"

Margaret put her back to the door and said, "It's very serious, I'm afraid. I'll just wait for the doctor."

The housekeeper's face set in stubborn lines. She stood like a stork, first on one foot, then the other.

Fortunately, the doctor came quickly. Plump as a pear, a gold watch chain dangling on his half-buttoned vest, he opened the door officiously and bent over Budge's contorted body. He felt for a pulse, then pried open the right hand and extracted the little box.

"A case for the police, I'm afraid. Possible suicide." He turned to Mrs. Millet, the box on the palm of his hand, the word POISON clearly visible. "Are you a relative, Madam?"

"Oh, no, I'm just on the same tour. But suicide?" She shook her head. "That box is his, though. He kept some sort of natural laxative in it."

"Is that so? Well, I expect the police will want to hear about it—did you find the body?"

"No, my friend, Mrs. Hark. She's the one who saw... She's in the lounge, downstairs. She nearly fainted."

The housekeeper squirmed half into the room, and got her first good look at Budge's remains. She yelped and threw her apron over her face, wailing "Oi, the poor man! the poor man! It's 'orrible! 'Orrible!" She raved on, making the dramatic most of Budge's demise. Margaret hoped she was satisfied.

Doctor Harris locked the door and went to call the police. Margaret went to the bus to tell Sybil. In just a few minutes, a police car arrived and shortly afterward, a uniformed policeman came out and said, "Everybody stay on the bus. Chief Inspector Nail will be with you shortly. No one is allowed to leave." He stood by the bus door to make sure.

Immediately, Sybil had her hands full.

"What's it got to do with us?" Freddie Factor demanded, and while the other passengers might not have put it so crudely, there was general agreement. Where was Mrs. Hark? Why was she allowed off the bus, when the others had to stay?

At the height of the clamor, the Chief Inspector appeared, a big, burly man with a flourishing moustache. He stepped into the bus. "A member of your tour is dead, under suspicious circumstances. This is a serious matter—a possible homicide."

The passengers gasped in horror and clamored anew. Was there a homicidal maniac loose in Penzance? Were they in danger of their lives?

"Quiet, please!" the Chief Inspector glared them to silence. "I'm sorry for the interruption to your holiday, but we'll have to take statements. Perhaps your tour guide," he smiled into Sybil's anxious face, "can find you a more comfortable place than the bus, but I need your passports and your luggage, which will be searched. Please try to remember anything you know or have observed about the victim... Mr. er... Budge. Anything at all, whether it seems important or not. And be prepared to tell us what you did last night and when you last saw the deceased."

Homicide or no homicide, the travelers were indignant in several languages. Margaret nodded; she hadn't believed the doctor's suicide theory and was glad the police didn't, either. But poor, ordinary Budge, who would want to do him in?

She eyed her fellow tourists one by one, registering their behavior at the news. The Quists, that closely united couple, had turned to each other in distress, but their words told her they only regretted the delay and the possible loss of their scheduled time in London. Jake Arvin seemed to agree with the protesters, saying "That's right!" and "You said it, they can't do this!" and "We're American citizens." Then Molly handed him his video camera, and he taped the excitement for his travelogue. How callous people were when the misfortunes of others impinged upon their own convenience!

Curiously, Goldy Greening was silent. Margaret expected her to complain loudest of all, but there she sat, looking sallow and sick, her painted face suddenly old under the orange hair. She was the only one on the bus, except for Margaret herself, who seemed to mind that Tony Budge had lost his life.

Grunt Davis sat impassively at Goldy's side, never taking his deep-set eyes from her face, waiting to be told how he felt.

Sybil and Malcolm went to telephone. When they returned, Sybil said, "We're going back to the Monarch. They've agreed to let us write out our statements in the ballroom."

By police permission, Margaret stayed with Judy at the Pettit, and the manager escorted them back to their room. Judy was still shaky. Doctor Harris gave her a mild sedative, saying the police could talk to her later, when she'd recovered from the shock.

"You wouldn't believe the way those people carried on," Margaret said, when they were finally alone. "And the hotel maid..." She described the woman's behavior in scathing terms. Her object, of course, was to convince Judy that her own weakness was minor and perfectly natural.

Stretched out on the unmade bed, Judy said drowsily, "To think I hardly noticed him. What could have made anybody want to kill him?"

"Exactly what I thought. A postal clerk, who liked to travel on his vacations. Unless... unless he wasn't."

"Margaret! Oh, it's fantastic. Why do they think it was murder? Why not food poisoning, or something? But he'd have made a perfect spy, wouldn't he? So... so anonymous."

"The doctor thought it was suicide—with poison from that little box."

"What little box?"

"The stuff he gave Freddie for a laxative, remember? When he died, the box was in his hand."

"Oh, yes, Freddie, in the New Forest. Of course I remember. Ruined my lunch." Judy hitched herself up on the bedstead and stuffed a pillow behind her head. "Freddie. If it was really poison, he had some of it. I thought he looked like a crook. Of all the things I imagined though, Tony Budge getting himself killed wasn't in it."

"Yes... I feel that way, too. Darn it, I liked him! He was so proud of his travels and all the places he'd been. It's cruel. He could have seen something, I suppose, or even been involved, himself. Remember how he ducked when Jake was using his camera? And he was secretive about that package he got at the post office. Wonder what it was?"

"And when Davis said 'He's twigged!' it could have been Budge he meant." Judy struggled to stave off sleep. "Goldy Greening! Wait a minute—there's something, what is it? The first day, on the bus... yes, I remember!" She told Margaret how Budge had dropped a scrap of yellow paper as he boarded the bus, and Goldy Greening had caught it and crumpled it in her hand.

"Oh, but it's all so far fetched, Margaret. At least we're not going to get involved, like we did in Texas. What will Willy say? Oh, I hope he doesn't hear about this! Do you think I should try to call home?"

Judy Hark was wrong when she said "we're not going to get involved." When the police searched the luggage, they found Budge's satchel, emptied and flattened, crammed into Judy's largest suitcase. Quite a coincidence, since she had also found the body.

Chapter 13
Mrs. Hark: Whose Side Are We On?

Judy Hark stared at the bleak, mustard-colored walls of the back room in the Penzance Police Station and wondered what she had done in her past lives to deserve this. To be questioned in this manner, by these two stern-faced men, was outside her life-long experience, various as that had been. The big man was the worst, although he was older and should have known better. He seemed to really think she was a murderer, and he had only to catch her out. The younger man wore a poker face, but didn't appear to have judged her in advance. His face was rather nice, in fact, with mild blue eyes that questioned instead of condemning.

Margaret Millet sat beside her, on the questionee's side of a long, formica-topped table. A uniformed policewoman stood by the door, and a tape recorder hummed, recording every word, cough, and rustle of movement. Tony Budge's tan satchel, flattened and empty, sat in the center of the table. The white box marked "POISON" lay beside it.

"I'm Chief Inspector Nail, and this is Inspector Lamb of Scotland Yard," the big man began. "I called in the Yard right off, the deceased being a foreigner and all." He glowered as though he regretted the necessity.

"Now then, Mrs. Hark, this satchel was found in your suitcase. How did it get there?"

"I have no idea. If it's Budge's satchel, the last time I saw it was in the limo that took us from the Monarch to the Pettit Hotel."

"It wasn't in your suitcase this morning, when you packed?"

"Certainly not."

"And when did you last see your suitcase?"

"I put it in the hall for pick up a little before seven this morning. And it was locked."

"So someone else got into your suitcase, after seven this morning..."

"They must have. Was the suitcase locked when you searched it?" Clumsy policemen rummaging through my personal belongings, wrinkling all the lovely new clothes I bought especially for the trip! Judy's blood pressure rose like a rocket. And a murderer opened my suitcase to plant false evidence! That's worse.

"I'll ask the questions, Mrs. Hark." Chief Inspector Nail switched his attention to the little white box. "Do you recognize this box? Dr. Harris said you could identify it."

Margaret answered that one. "Yes. Budge had it out at lunch one day. Some sort of natural laxative, he said, safe in small doses but poisonous if you took too much. Is that what killed him? The doctor said it might be suicide."

"We don't have that information yet," Nail said. And wouldn't say if we did, his manner implied. He went on in menacing tones, "It's been my experience that very few men write jolly postcards to their mothers and wash out their shorts just before they take poison. Mr. Budge was almost certainly murdered."

"Well, ask Freddie Factor," Judy snapped. "Budge gave Freddie some of that stuff; we saw him."

"He called it Barbados purge nuts," Margaret said. "I remember the name because I went to Barbados once, on a Caribbean cruise. Yes, ask Freddie about it."

"We will do, never fear. Which one is Freddie Factor?"

"He shared Budge's seat on the bus," Judy said. "They weren't together, though. They had separate hotel rooms."

Inspector Lamb, a silent observer to that point, asked, "What did Mr. Budge keep in the satchel; can you tell us?"

"I don't really know. His camera equipment—oh, and he picked up a package at the post office. He put that in the satchel, I think. I wasn't paying much attention; I was tired and wanted to get to the hotel."

Lamb shifted his gaze. "Did you notice a package, Mrs. Millet?"

"Yes, I did. Mr. Budge had been looking for mail every place the tour stopped, and I asked him if the package was what he'd been waiting for. It was about this size," she sketched it with her hands, "and looked lumpy, as though it wasn't a box, but just something wrapped in padding, or thicknesses of paper. There were lots of stamps on it—but I only got a glimpse. He was very quick to put it in the satchel."

"The size... can you estimate it in inches?"

"About the size of a brick, maybe eight inches long by four inches wide. Not quite two inches thick—but that's just an impression. I can't be sure."

Chief Inspector Nail, the British bulldog, had not given up his line of questioning. "And you didn't see Budge again, Mrs. Hark, after the limo ride to the Pettit? You were tired. Did you go straight to bed?"

Trying to trip me up. "Not straight to bed. I ordered tea, rested a while, then took a shower and washed out some things. Then I went to bed."

"And never left your room until the next morning."

"That's right."

"And what did you do, Mrs. Millet?"

"Oh... I went out to see the town."

Inspector Lamb showed interest, and questioned Margaret until he had the whole story of her evening with Malcolm. "Is it usual for the bus driver to entertain a member of the tour?"

"A bus driver is a human being, Inspector. I'm sure he would rather have spent his evening with our tour guide, but she was otherwise occupied last night." Margaret seemed about to say more, then blinked and closed her lips firmly.

"Yes, I've met your tour guide." A joyous smile splintered Lamb's poker face, and for a moment he looked boyish and charming. (The Sybil Darington Effect, Judy said to herself. Even policemen are not immune.) It was only a moment. Lamb's face turned doubly stern and expressionless as he discarded the thought of Sybil and went on. "And you last saw Mr. Budge when?"

"At the Monarch before dinner," Margaret said. "Budge, Freddie Factor, and I went to the Monarch in the limo. Then I met Malcolm and went off. I didn't see Mr. Budge again. When I got back to the room, Judy was sound asleep. Oh, and there was a letter for me on the dresser. When did that come, Judy?"

"A letter, Mrs. Hark?"

"Oh, yes. The man said he brought it over from the Monarch. I didn't see him—he slipped it through the mail slot—but I spoke to him. It must have been about nine o'clock."

The ladies were unshakable, and their stories varied not at all under repeated questioning. After they described finding the body six or seven times, the policemen asked for all sorts of background information about their homes, relatives, and friends. The more they asked, the angrier Judy Hark became.

At last, Chief Inspector Nail growled, "That's all for now. You both claim you never saw Budge before this trip, but we'll be checking that, and if there's a connection, we'll find it, I promise you. You'd do better to tell us now. It'll look bad for you, if we find something ourselves."

That did it. "Are you threatening us?" Judy took a deep breath and let herself go. "Well, let me give you one more reference to check. You just contact Sheriff's Deputy C.D. Townley, in Big Bend, Texas, if you want to know what kind of citizens we are. He had a murder on his hands too, and we helped him find the killer. Just you ask Crawdad Townley!" Her face burned, and she instantly regretted saying they had been involved in murder before.

Margaret clapped her hands and crowed, "Good for you, Judy!"

"May we go, now?" Judy's voice would have frozen a hot spring in mid bubble.

Late that afternoon, the tour group bused across the Cornish peninsula to the north shore, where accommodations had been arranged at the Poldenna Castle in St. Ives.

"One has to admire the staff work," Margaret said. "Where was it we were supposed to be tonight?"

"Lynton, 'in the heart of Lorna Doone country.'"

Indeed, Sybil and Gateway World had done wonders. To Judy's relief, even the police realized the tourists couldn't stay in Penzance with no hotel rooms, and their limited travel time slipping away. The tour would continue—with Inspector Christopher Lamb along. Chief Inspector Nail was left to deal with the Penzance end of the investigation, and Scotland Yard, as Lamb had told them, would check for a tourist with a criminal background or some connection to Tony Budge.

Because the tourists had spent the day with the police, they would spend the night in St. Ives and catch up to schedule on Day Six. They'd still see and explore the ruins at Tintagel, but would take the main highway to Bath and skip Glastonbury, Wells, and the Cheddar Gorge.

Sybil explained this on the way to St. Ives, stressing the positive. Her eyes were shadowed, and the hand holding the microphone trembled, but she stood as straight as ever, and her fluted tones carried bravely through the bus.

"We've been incredibly lucky to find rooms at Poldenna Castle. Actually, their summer season is over, and they are preparing for winter boarders, but they'll have us as a special favor. Please be patient—they have already reduced staff, and service may be a little slow."

"Sounds like Poldenna Castle is run the same way I run my beach cottages," Margaret said.

Judy asked, "Isn't there a riddle about St. Ives? How does it go? 'As I was going to St. Ives, I met a man with seven wives...

and every wife had seven...' something."

"Right. It ends, 'how many were going to St. Ives?'"

"Forty seven. Plus a hard-working staff of two and a policeman," Judy said.

She was quite recovered from the physical effects of finding Tony Budge's body. Dr. Harris's medicine and a nap had done much to restore her, followed by the Pettit's nourishing soup and coffee so good it was probably French. Not that she would ever forget what she had seen—Budge's dead face was the stuff of nightmares.

The police had stopped short of reading her rights and charging her with murder, but only just. She had been fingerprinted! Her fingers still bore traces of ink. She looked across the aisle; the Australian teacher sitting there had inky fingers too, which was somehow a comfort. How could that Chief Inspector Nail suspect her? Perfectly maddening. She resolved to put the police station experience behind her and observe what was going on in the bus.

Christopher Lamb leaned back in his seat and watched Sybil as though unable to look at anything else. Judy could see him, in the aisle seat poor Tony Budge would have used, by turning her head to the left. Due to the daily seat rotation, she and Margaret were now half way forward on the right side of the bus, with Lamb and Freddie behind them, a reversal that happened when they went around the bus's back end.

The Quists were along the same line of vision, across the aisle and one row back from Inspector Lamb. Victor held Vicky's hand, his shoulder touching hers, and they looked out the window together.

Goldy Greening and her beefy companion had rotated to the last seat on the left side of the bus. Goldy met Judy's gaze with a sickly smile and seemed to have lost her sparkle, though bediamonded as usual. The way the bus swayed back there—Judy wondered if Goldy suffered from motion sickness.

Jake and Molly Arvin sat near the front. Jake hunched low

in his seat and she couldn't tell what they were doing, but the video camera didn't seem to be in use.

She had to twist her neck to see Freddie, who squirmed and grinned directly behind her. Anyone would think he'd been especially chosen to sit with the policeman and help on the case. Judy snorted in scorn. When one really helped the police, as she knew first-hand, one didn't play for attention.

The bus passed through the streets of St. Ives and climbed steeply. Poldenna Castle faced north, overlooking St. Ives Bay, and castle it was. Expansions had been added, but the main building rose in solid stone, with a crenelated roof line and square towers.

They entered the great hall, heated by a huge stone fireplace. Oak paneling surrounded the registration desk, where a cheerful woman in black sorted keys.

"Dinner at seven in the dining room," she said. "I'll have your luggage sent up straight away." She offered registration cards and accepted passports from Inspector Lamb.

"Glad to see my passport again," Margaret said. "I feel naked without it. Do you plan to keep them much longer?"

Lamb said, "The Yard is checking identities. We should be able to give most of them back in the morning."

Pretty fast, Judy thought; the wonders of modern communication.

Their room overlooked the castle's brilliant gardens, the fishing boats of St. Ives harbor, and the bay. A short distance below the garden, nearly hidden by vines and trees, a most intriguing structure clung to the hillside.

"Look, Margaret... what do you suppose that is? That queer little stone house?"

Margaret joined her at the window and looked down on the slate roof and granite walls of the small, square building. "Like a secret hideaway," she said. "I don't think you could see it at all, except from above."

"There's a path, though. Let's take a walk before dinner—if

the police will let us out."

"Yes, let's."

Margaret checked the adjoining bathroom and came out gleefully waving a white washcloth. Judy snatched it with joy and buried her face in the soft cotton loops. So far, washcloths had not been furnished by the English hotels, not even the Monarch, and the one she kept in a plastic bag in her suitcase was beginning to hum.

Chapter 14
Mrs. Millet: The Word From Texas

"Here's our luggage," Margaret called to Judy, who was in the bathroom having a good wash. The suitcases had arrived on a trolley, rolled along the hallway by an ancient retainer. Such was his haste that he didn't wait for a tip, but dumped the luggage off, rapped sharply, and pushed the cart on to the next door.

"Now we'll see what it's like to have your things searched by the police." Margaret hoisted her suitcase onto the bed. Not as bad as she expected. Things definitely gone through and out of place, but all in all, the repacking was a fairly neat job.

Judy emerged from the bathroom, refreshed and full of vim. "Unlocked! I knew it!" She opened her suitcase on the other bed, thumbing the catches triumphantly. "And look at the scratches! Any policeman worth his salt would know those locks were forced! See, Margaret?"

Yes, there were scratches and one catch was bent. Of course luggage does get abused in the course of a long trip. "Mine was unlocked, too," Margaret said. "I guess a suitcase lock is no barrier to the police—or anybody else, for that matter. Can you see where the satchel was?" Judy's clothes were squashed and rumpled much more than her own. When they found the satchel, the police must have examined every garment down to its seams.

After hanging up clothes for the next day and repacking the

rest, the ladies strolled downstairs and out the main door of Poldenna Castle, with no let or hindrance. A cool breeze from the sea came over the rooftops of St. Ives, lifting Margaret's spirits as it ruffled her hair. The gardens still bloomed, in the manner of English gardens, even in October. She looked for the path they had seen from above.

"Here." A break in the boxwood hedge. The path was broad and well traveled, probably the standard way to town for those on foot.

And she had been right; the tiny stone house could not be seen from the path. She pushed into a tangle of elder brush and wild blackberry where the house should be, taking a painful scratch on one arm in the process. Yes, there it was, behind a crumbling picket fence. Judy pushed close, looking over her shoulder.

"Look—a name plate on the fence." Margaret tugged the ivy aside and read the name aloud, loving the Englishness of it. "Fealty Cottage." Houses had names in England, and you could get your mail by using them, even though the name gave no clue to the house's location. Attractive as it looked, Margaret couldn't get to Fealty Cottage without serious risk to skin and clothing. She backed carefully out of the wild growth and retreated to the open path. Judy followed.

The sun was setting in a flaming damask sky, the colors reflected in the gentle waves of St. Ives Bay. "Gorgeous!" Judy revolved to take it all in. "No wonder somebody built a castle here."

A stick broke with a sharp crack on the path behind them. Margaret stiffened. Had someone followed them? Suddenly, she wished herself in a well lighted room, any well lighted room, not on this dim, woodsy path under the sunset sky. She moved close to Judy and they edged toward the elder bushes. Heavy footsteps crunched toward them.

"Freddie!" Judy almost shouted. "You gave us a scare!"

Freddie jumped. He hadn't seen them and he was nervous,

too. "Oh, there you are. I wanted to talk to you ladies—saw you leave the lobby, and thought we might have a little confab, you know?"

He had followed them. "Well, here we are. What's on your mind?" Margaret had no desire to talk to Freddie, but the reverse might be interesting. Judy waited in silent disdain.

"I understand you ladies found poor old Budge. Sure sorry you were the ones—I feel bad that I didn't go looking for him when Beauchus asked me to."

An apology. Well, Freddie had a lot to apologize for.

Judy said, "I'm sorry, too. Her name is Sybil—or you could call her Miss Darington."

Freddie threw up a hand to defend himself. "Okay, I get the point. I'm a pretty crude guy, sometimes—but I don't mean any harm. Give me a break. I just wondered... well, about that package Budge picked up at the post office. Have the police found it, d'you know? They asked me a lot of questions about that and that satchel he carried. And I thought, maybe... Do you think he was a smuggler? Was his room torn up—you know, like somebody was lookin' for something? Do you think he was killed for that package?"

Margaret said, "Freddie, how would we know? And why should we worry about it? That's for the police to deal with. I've no idea what was in that package."

Freddie was unsnubbable. "I thought you might have found something extra in a suitcase."

Judy picked him up sharply. "Something extra in a suitcase! What are you trying to say?"

"Or something missing? But I don't think... not a hotel thief... well, I dunno."

Margaret took a stern line. "Freddie, did you see someone fooling with our suitcases? Answer me, Freddie. It might be very important."

"Not that night—it's probably nothing to do with Budge. But, yeah, I saw somebody by your door, early this morning. I was coming down the stairs and I just stopped and waited 'til the coast was clear. Didn't want to get in a hassle, see?"

"Who, Freddie? Was it someone from the tour? Did you recognize...?"

Freddie pouted like a stubborn child. "If nothing was gone or put in, maybe I'd better not say. Why should I get somebody in trouble—have the cops asking more questions? Maybe I imagined the whole thing."

What an impossible creature. "Why are you doing this? If you won't say who you saw, why tell us anything?"

"Maybe later." Evasive, sly. "Maybe I'll just check it out first." He turned away, muttering something that sounded like "check da tree, I..." Waving a hand behind him, Freddie scuttled back toward the hotel.

"Well! What do you make of that? Did he see who put the satchel in my suitcase—or did he put it there himself? He had the best chance of anybody; he was staying at the Pettit. And he had some of that poison stuff, too! I'll bet he's the one, and trying to find out if the police found the satchel and what they did about it."

Margaret shook her head. "Freddie, a cold-blooded poisoner? I don't know—he's sneaky, but... A thief, that I could believe. Some of what he said sounded true, though. I think he did see somebody." A cold shiver shook her body. Should they have told Freddie about the satchel and warned him that whoever he saw could be the murderer?

"Let's go back, Judy. The wind's turning cold."

The next morning, Margaret circled the breakfast buffet in the Poldenna Castle's dining room and filled a bowl with assorted cereal flakes, dried fruits, nuts, and seeds, trying to duplicate the granola she made at home. There was rich cream too, and it made a change from the English breakfast of bacon, sausage, eggs, and grilled tomatoes.

She joined Judy at a table by the window and poured her

first cup of tea. The Poldenna Castle knew how to take care of guests, no question. Besides furnishing that (in England) endangered specie, the wash cloth, the beds had been billowy clouds, the bath tub deep enough to launch ships, and the water soft and hot.

"I could stay here forever." She looked out to the bright garden and the turquoise sea beyond. "Let the tour go on without me."

"It is beautiful," Judy said. "And we've had wonderful weather, haven't we? I'd soon miss California, though, wouldn't you?"

"I suppose so, in time. But Judy, in spite of everything, I feel like I've come home. Like this is my native land." She would have said more, but the approach of Inspector Lamb cut her short. Was he going to join them? He was.

"May I join you, ladies?" A humble request. He waited for their reply, his slender height bending, almost bowing, in courtesy.

"Of course." Judy indicated the chair beside her.

Lamb put down his plate, sat, and turned a teacup on its saucer. Before pouring tea, he pulled a folded, brownish paper from an inside jacket pocket. "Something you might like to see." He handed it to Judy.

Judy read with crinkled eyes and snorts of delight, then passed the paper to Margaret.

A report from the United States, from Brewster County, Texas, from Deputy Sheriff C.D. Townley. The original had been hand-written on Sheriff's Department stationery, in bold, well-formed, Palmer-method script, clear and readable even after two faxings.

"Margaret Millet and Judy Hark—They wouldn't kill nobody, that's silly. If you all are lucky enough to have these two mixed in with your suspects, count your blessings. They are sharp as needles, curious as monkeys, and people tell them all sorts of things. What they don't get told, they figure out. You Limeys be nice to them or I, Personal, will come over there and knock your heads together. Signed, C.D. Townley, Sheriff's Deputy, Brewster County, Texas, U.S.A."

The document moved Margaret to tears. "Don't you wish he was here? Couldn't we just use ol' Crawdad Townley on this trip?" She gave it back to Lamb reluctantly, longing to keep it for a souvenir. If Crawdad Townley were only here and in charge of the case! What a lot they would have to tell him, and to ask about. Freddie, Goldy Greening, Richard Darington (who had been in Penzance the night of the murder!)—they could have told Crawdad all their wild surmises, asked all their silly questions. She looked at Christopher Lamb, wondering if he would listen to two old ladies.

As though he heard her thoughts, he said, "I'm afraid I'll have to do." He added, "It seems we owe you an apology, Mrs. Hark. You have checked out in every way, and we've found no connection with Anthony Budge or any criminal background. The lock on your suitcase had been forced, just as you suggested. Please let me say, for Scotland Yard and the Penzance Police Department, that we are very sorry for any distress we may have caused you."

Well, that was handsome, Margaret thought. I do like a man who knows how to admit when he's wrong. Lamb seemed younger and better looking than he had in the Penzance police station.

"Apology accepted," Judy said. "Really you couldn't be blamed, under the circumstances."

Lamb grinned broadly and said, "That report made my day. I can't wait for Chief Inspector Nail to see it."

Judy laughed and the three of them finished breakfast amicably. Margaret did notice that their customary tablemates shunned them. The Arvins sat as far away as they could get, and Freddie put his head in the door, looked around, and went out again, presumably to find his breakfast elsewhere. It's the company we keep, she thought. Policemen are not popular. What a pity.

Chapter 15
Mrs. Hark: Alibis

Judy Hark ran a forefinger under the waistband of her trim black trousers and decided not to eat lunch. The English breakfasts made themselves felt. When the bus pulled into Tintagel, she only wanted to explore on foot, and had no desire to visit the kiosk selling Cornish pasties.

She also saw no need to get involved with Inspector Lamb. Why was Margaret sticking so closely to his side? In spite of his apology, Judy still felt the insult she had suffered. Was she really free from suspicion, or did he say so in hopes she would give herself away? For that matter, could Lamb speak for Scotland Yard and the Penzance Police? Would Chief Inspector Nail concur in his apology? She needed to think about these things.

Across from the Cornish pasties, a battered Land Rover offered rides. Its driver barked, "Ride to the ruins, fifty pence. Home of King Arthur. Tintagel—rhymes with fragile—ride to the ruins. Eleventh century ruins on top of fourth century ruins, may have been King Arthur's Camelot. Hop in now, almost ready to go..."

"I think I will," Judy told Margaret. "How long will we be here?" This to Malcolm, who had helped them out of the bus.

"About an hour. Plenty of time—but the ruins are just down that gully. Easy walking distance."

"Oh. In that case, I'll walk. Coming, Margaret?"

"Don't you want to try a Cornish pastie?" Margaret had

breakfasted on dried fruits, nuts, and cereal flakes, and had no waistline to worry about, anyway. "You go ahead. I'll get a pastie and follow." Most of the tour group agreed with Margaret and gathered round the pastie stall.

Judy picked her way down the steep gully where the Land Rover had gone. The morning sea fog had lifted in a stiff breeze but showed no sign of letting the sun through. It might even rain. She scanned the sky to assess the thickening overcast.

The gully opened out on a rocky flat where the Land-Rover had turned and parked, pointed back the way it came. Its passengers were climbing a promontory above the sea, calling and pulling each other over the hard places. The low walls of the ruins stood above, outlined against thick, gray clouds.

The waters of a small cove lapped the base of the promontory. Judy walked to the water's edge, noting a cave in the cliffs, revealed by the ebbing tide. On her right, a bench stood on a wide ledge, thoughtfully placed for viewing the ruins and the breakers that crashed into the cove from the sea.

How impregnable King Arthur's castle (if it was King Arthur's castle) must have been on that cliff top. The approaches from land and sea were steep, with no cover whatever. The cove, completely hidden until one got very close, must have been ideal for smugglers. She opened her camera and photographed the ruins against the sky, the half submerged cave, and the path climbing the cliff, complete with climbers. Then shivering a little in the salty breeze, she pulled her hand-knit sweater close about her and perched on the bench to await Margaret's arrival. They could go up to the ruins if Margaret wanted to climb, or just look at them from the bench.

Margaret did not appear, but Sybil Darington rapidly approached, almost running as though in flight. When she saw the bench was occupied she slowed her pace and tossed back her wind-blown hair.

"Hello, Mrs. Hark. Grand view, isn't it?"

"Out of the wind, too." Judy moved over on the bench.

Sybil's face was decidedly wan. Once seated, she had no small talk. Her travel guide smile slipped away, and she gazed out to sea, her perfect features dreamy and sad.

Judy said the first thing that came to mind. Actually, the thing in her mind when Sybil turned up. "At first, the police thought I murdered Tony Budge. They found his satchel stuffed into my suitcase."

"Oh, Mrs. Hark!" That woke the dreamer. "How could they think such a thing—oh, surely not!"

"Well, I found the body. And I have no alibi—Margaret was out having a good time, but I was so tired that night, I stayed in and went to bed and of course, I can't prove it."

"But I sent you to find him. For that matter, I have no alibi either. I had dinner at the Monarch, but there's nobody to vouch for me after that."

"They grilled me at the police station in Penzance." Judy grimaced. "Grilled" was the word. She had felt like an unfortunate fish, caught and seared over a campfire. "Have you been questioned, too?"

"We all wrote out what we'd done that night..." Anxiety flattened Sybil's voice. "I just said I was in my room at the Monarch. They can't prove I wasn't... can they?"

Judy could hear her son Johnny, age four, saying "You didn't see me do it, did you?" She could always tell when Johnny lied to her.

"And where were you really, Sybil? With Richard?"

"With Richard! Whatever gave you that idea?"

Judy met Sybil's gray blue eyes. A question is no answer, she thought, but it's better than a lie. "Margaret saw his car, parked on a side street. What was he doing in Penzance?"

"Oh, God! Have you told the police? Oh, Mrs. Hark, he didn't do anything—I've got to keep him out of this; he just mustn't get involved in it, don't you see? Not after being tried for our robbery—they'll pounce on him at once, if there's any way to pull him into it!"

Sybil had been cynical about Richard before, but here was sisterly feeling for the family black sheep, after all. Glad to see it, Judy softened.

"No, we haven't told the police. At least, not so far. Why don't you tell me about it. If there's no need for them to know, I don't see why we should say anything."

Sybil sighed, her defenses crumbling. "I've been frantic. Richard and I—we've always fought, you see. Whenever we get together, we fight. A few minutes in the same room, and we start shouting at each other like characters in a Neil Simon play—it's awful. Nobody else can make me do that, but Richard can. He's not a murderer, though. Stupid, greedy, easily led, a complete fool, but not a murderer. And he's in trouble—terrible trouble—and not just with the police."

"What kind of trouble? Can we help?"

"Nobody can help... I'm so muddled and confused." Sybil clenched her fists and stared out over the tumbling waters of Tintagel Cove. The silence lengthened. Judy waited.

At last, Sybil spoke. "Richard parked his caravan in a camp near Penzance, and that's where he's staying. We met after dinner, at a pub down by the front. I asked him about Goldy Greening and what he was mixed up in, but he wouldn't tell me anything then; just said 'ask me no questions' and bragged that he'd soon have plenty of money, and I could quit my job. 'Quit nursing the wrinklers 'round our magic isle,' he said. He's dreadful—please, Mrs. Hark, don't be offended."

"I suppose I am a wrinkler, but I can't say I care for the term. No matter. Richard, too, will get old. Do go on."

"I went back to the hotel about eleven o'clock. So I really was there the rest of the night..."

"And?" Obviously, there was more.

"Well, I didn't sleep very well." Sybil hesitated and searched Judy's face once again. Judy knew what she was thinking; should she say more? could this person be trusted? wouldn't it be better to say nothing at all?

"No, it wouldn't," Judy said. "Let's have the rest of it. A worry shared is a worry halved, they say."

Sybil lowered her eyes. "You're right, of course. If you'd been there, you'd understand. He couldn't have been so devastated—he wouldn't have even come to me—if he'd committed murder. But he saw the body."

"Richard saw the body? He was there?"

"Yes. He knocked on my door about 3:00 A.M. He was in a terrible state—complete panic. He'd gone to see Tony Budge and found him dead on the floor. The door was on the latch; he just walked in and saw the body lying there. He said he didn't touch anything—just stood there. Then he shut the door and it locked—and he ran away and came to me."

"I see. He was afraid to call the police."

"Yes. I said, was he sure it was murder? Couldn't the man just have died? And he said it was murder, all right. He said Budge was carrying jewels. Budge was in with a gang of jewel thieves, the same ones who robbed our house, and he carried the loot. Richard said either somebody killed him to get the jewels, or the gang killed him because he was 'skimming,' selling some of them himself instead of delivering them as he was supposed to."

"And how did Richard know all this?"

"That's when he told me about Goldy Greening. She's the boss of the gang. She operates by striking up an acquaintance with someone in the house—the house they plan to rob. It's all very carefully done, and she's miles away when the robbery happens."

"What was she doing on this tour, then?"

"That's how Richard found her and cooked up his great plan for getting rich. It's complicated, rather..." Sybil straightened and looked over Judy's shoulder. Footsteps crunched in the gravel. Someone was coming.

"Oh, Mrs. Hark, please don't say a word. You won't, will you? I can't tell you any more now—we've got to get back to the bus."

Margaret hove into view, munching around the edges of a paper-wrapped lump that disintegrated in her hands as she chewed. "There you are!" she called gaily. "This thing is so hot, I can hardly eat it. Have you been up to the top?"

Sybil managed a smile and a greeting, and fled.

"What's the matter with her? Oh dear, have I interrupted a therapy session again? Here, let me sit. My pastie is falling apart."

"Pastie? Is that how you say it?"

"Yes. Pastie, to rhyme with nasty. It's kind of a meat-pie-to-go. I waited ages to get it, and then they cooked it so long in the microwave that it practically dissolved." She nibbled a little more, then rose and shook the crumbled mess out of its paper wrapping, into the cove. "Food for the fishes."

After Tintagel, the day went down hill. A long, long, bus ride on the main roads. Sybil did her best to amuse them with stories and music tapes, but it was a tired, grumpy group that got off the bus to tour the Roman spa in the city called Bath.

Inspector Lamb skipped the Roman baths and Judy didn't see him again until just before dinner at the hotel, when he pushed into the lobby with a briefcase and a worried frown.

The ladies had come down early and occupied two of the comfortable lobby chairs. Judy was reading a newspaper with considerable interest when Lamb addressed them.

"Mrs. Millet, Mrs. Hark—I wonder if you could help me. I'm in a bit of a spot." He smiled hesitantly, uncertain of his reception. Margaret lifted her expressive eyebrows and smiled. Judy glanced at him and returned to the paper. Let Margaret deal with the policeman.

"It's the tour guide, Miss Darington. I need to question her further..." He flushed in embarrassment. "Since she's alone, I wonder if you'd mind... that is, perhaps I could talk to her in your room?"

Judy eyed his red face. He didn't trust himself to be alone with

Sybil. The man had a bad case, and was handicapped severely by his ideas of proper behavior for a gentleman who was also a policeman. How delightful! She and Margaret could watch him work—and squirm.

Margaret said, "Of course, Inspector. We'd be happy to help. We've become quite well acquainted with Sybil, and I'm sure she's eager to give you any information she can."

Judy spoke sharply. "Sybil didn't kill anybody. You're not going to badger her like you did me, are you?"

A question like "have you stopped beating your wife?" Lamb answered in some confusion. "It's only routine... uh, some points she may be able to clear up for us... things that need to be checked."

"Then that's all right. When do you want to come?"

"After dinner, please."

This was agreed, and the dinner gong ended the discussion. Judy held back until Lamb left them and then said, "Margaret, there's quite a lot you should know before we see that man again. I promised Sybil I wouldn't tell, but surely she didn't mean you—and we don't want her in trouble with the police."

"I thought so," Margaret said.

Chapter 16
Mrs. Millet: Inspector Lamb Interrogates

Tintagel had disappointed Margaret Millet, and not just because of the Cornish pastie. The travel schedule touted it "...birthplace of King Arthur; explore his ruined castle..." but Margaret knew perfectly well that fourth century Tintagel was not King Arthur's, but the castle of King Mark of Cornwall, site of the legend of Tristram and Isoud. (She owned a copy of *The Enchanted Cup*, a well researched modern language version of the legend by Dorothy James Roberts.)

Just off Tintagel Head lay the island where Tristram had his first Knightly battle against the Irish Marhaus. Roberts had written of the Marhaus, "...he himself admits he is the greatest champion in Christendom which means, once you have translated it out of Irish, that he is a good man with the spear and sword."

Margaret had looked out to sea and tried to feel what she should feel at treading the ground where Isoud paced, waiting for Tristram, her one true love, but it was hard going. For one thing, there was no time; the bus would soon depart. Then it started to rain, so they rode the Land Rover back to the car park, meekly paying their fifty-pence pieces for two minutes of damp transportation.

Here in Bath, however, Christopher Lamb wanted them to sit in while he interrogated Sybil, and Judy obviously had news to impart. This was more like it. At dinner, Margaret disposed of her bean soup and Cornish hen in record time. When Judy showed a tendency to linger over Bath buns and tea, she sent such meaningful glances that Victor Quist, sitting on her left, asked, "What are you ladies doing tonight? Any plans?"

"Oh, no. It's been a long day. I have letters to write."

The Quists sat at this table because Jake and Molly Arvin had beaten them to their regular places. Freddie and Inspector Lamb occupied the other two chairs, and the rest of the tour dined pretty much as usual. Goldy Greening and her bodyguard sat by the window with an Oriental couple and a very elderly pair who were always the last ones on and off the bus and had to be helped on stairs. Sybil and Malcolm were elsewhere. They seldom dined with the group.

Judy rose, nodded to Chris Lamb, and headed for the elevators. Margaret said, "Excuse us," and followed.

Judy still carried the London newspaper she had been reading before dinner, having placed it under her chair during the meal. In their room, she handed it to Margaret. "Read that!" She pointed to a front-page headline.

"'Jewel Robbery. Wealthy Tycoon, Sir Augustus Cromarth, says priceless collection of historic gems stolen from Mayfair mansion' ...What does this have to do with anything? We may not have much time! Why don't you tell me about Sybil?"

"This is what it's all about! Budge was carrying the jewels from that robbery—that's what was in his package!"

Well! Judy has information I do not! Margaret perched on her bed to study the newspaper article more closely. The paper was two days old, and the time of the robbery did, indeed, make it possible that the loot had been mailed to Tony Budge. Rapturous descriptions of the gems were accompanied by smudgy photos that only gave the vaguest idea of their size and shape. When she had finished, Judy related everything she had learned from Sybil, and a good bit she had deduced on her own.

"So you see, Richard knew Goldy Greening before. She inveigled him into setting up the robbery at Darington Manor, and he probably got paid for it—robbing his own family! For Sybil's sake, let's hope the fire was something he didn't expect. Anyway, he's broke now. I don't know how he's involved in this new robbery, but he meant to profit by it. Sybil didn't have time to explain. Now Budge is dead, the jewels are gone, and Richard will be the first person Goldy Greening suspects, unless she killed Budge herself. But why would she? Budge was her own courier. Richard has good reason to be scared. Now—how much of this can we tell Inspector Lamb? We've got to decide before he and Sybil get here."

"And Goldy Greening's diamonds are real, after all," Margaret said.

Inspector Lamb had thoughtfully ordered after-dinner coffee sent to the ladies' room. The waiter placed the tray on the dresser and left them. Judy poured, setting out the hotel china, sturdy but of excellent quality, on a small round table next to the window. There were only three chairs, so Margaret made herself comfortable on the nearest bed, piled the pillows behind her back, and placed her cup and saucer on the night stand. Over Judy's shoulder, she could watch the faces of Sybil and Inspector Lamb.

Sybil sat ramrod straight and opened the conversation. "It's good of you, Mrs. Hark, to let us come here. I appreciate it." She had changed her tailored suit for black slacks and a silk blouse the color of Devonshire Cream. Her lovely face was pale and composed, and her remarkable eyes sought Judy's reassurance.

"Not at all; glad to help. I'm sure the Inspector just wants us to fill him in. After all, he just joined the tour, and knows very little about any of us. Isn't that right, Inspector?" Judy didn't intend to let Sybil be bullied.

Inspector Lamb took a deliberate sip of his coffee and looked around the room in a mild, inquiring way. "Of course. Just gathering information. Need all I can get." He sat behind the table with the closed window curtains at his back. When he slid his notebook onto the table top, his fingers brushed Sybil's hand. Margaret caught his reaction; the man actually blushed.

Lamb took something out of his briefcase and showed it to Sybil. "First, there's this little box marked 'POISON.' Can you tell me anything about it? Have you seen it before?"

Sybil shook her head, and Margaret remembered that Sybil stood behind Budge's chair while he explained the purge nuts to Freddie. Too bad. In the long run, honesty would be a better policy. She was about to speak up, but Judy saved her the trouble.

"We told you about that at the station. Budge carried some sort of laxative in it. He brought it out at lunch one day, when Freddie Factor was complaining about constipation. He gave some of the stuff to Freddie and said it was poisonous if you took too much; that was why he labeled the box that way. Is that what killed him?"

"Could be. We don't have the complete autopsy report yet, but the preliminary says severe gastric and intestinal distress." He referred to his notebook. "The stomach contents included heavy cream and bread, eaten just before death."

Margaret said, "Most of us bought cartons of Devonshire Cream, when we stopped in Widecombe."

"Not Budge, though," Judy put in. "Remember? We commented on it at the time, how he ate so much but didn't buy any to take with him. We decided he was too cheap."

"Can you remember who did? Buy the cream, I mean."

Margaret tried to visualize the line in the Roadside Cafe. "Just about everybody, I think. You'll have to ask them. Goldy Greening was just ahead of us in the line."

"Ah, yes, Mrs. Greening. A very interesting woman. Your brother Richard is acquainted with her, Miss Darington, isn't that so?" Lamb pounced—like a calm, gentle lion, claws retracted, fangs barely showing, a lion who could pin down his prey with words.

Sybil stiffened, breathed in, and said, "My brother has a wide acquaintance."

"Did you know Mrs. Greening before this tour?"

"No. And I wasn't aware that Richard did, either."

A careful truth. She may not have been aware before the tour, but she was now.

"Oh, yes. He was seen with her several times just before your home was robbed and burned. Mrs. Greening has a background of being acquainted with members of wealthy households that are subsequently robbed. We have quite a dossier on her at the Yard, but she's never been arrested—no tangible evidence, you see."

Margaret's opinion of Scotland Yard soared. They were already on the right track and wouldn't need the hints she had planned to drop. She decided to ask a few questions, instead. "Do you think Budge was involved in the Cromarth jewel robbery? Could he, for instance, have received the loot? That package he got in the mail—what was in it? Was it still in his room?"

Inspector Lamb drank some more coffee, taking his time. "Are all three of you undercover agents, then? I certainly came to the right place for information, didn't I?"

"Yes, you did. And there's another thing you should know. Judy, tell him what Freddie Factor said about seeing someone tamper with your suitcase."

"He didn't exactly say that. He hinted that he'd seen someone in the hall the morning after the murder. I think he was trying to find out what the police thought—and did—when they found Budge's satchel in my suitcase. Maybe he put it there himself. He stayed in the Pettit and had the best opportunity. Anybody else would have had to come back that morning."

Lamb thoughtfully rubbed his chin (clean shaven for the second time that day). "There's something in what you say, but Factor's alibi holds up pretty well. He was romancing a barmaid at the Monarch until closing time, 2:00 A.M."

"He didn't have to be there when Budge ate the poison. He could have left it and come back, stolen the jewels, and carried them off in the satchel." Margaret suddenly realized this could apply to any of them.

"We thought of that. The killer would take an awful risk that way, though. What if Budge was able to call for help before he died, and told someone who'd given him the dose? We think the murderer stayed to make sure Budge died." He wrote briefly in his notebook. "I'll talk to Factor about seeing someone in the hall, though. He didn't say who it was?"

"No." Freddie hadn't said who it was. He'd got all cagey and departed, muttering something about a tree. A tree! It didn't make sense.

Judy asked, "Will there be a funeral? In Penzance?"

"Budge's mother wants his body sent home. There'll be an inquest in Penzance. Several members of the tour will be requested to attend."

"Requested or required? When? We were going to spend a week in London right after the tour," Judy complained.

Lamb smiled a sweet, warm smile with his eyes on Sybil's face, and said "Required," as though it were a personal need. "Next Tuesday."

Recalling himself to duty, Lamb again consulted his notebook. "Three other items. Someone called the Pettit and asked for Budge's room number about 8:00 P.M. A man. We've asked all the men on the tour, but no results." He raised his eyebrows, but got no response.

"Number two: The tour company tried to call you that night at 10:15 but got no answer, Miss Darington. According to your statement, you didn't leave your room after dinner. Can you explain?"

"I was in the shower. I heard the telephone, but I let it ring."

A reasonable reply, very quickly supplied. She must have had it ready, Margaret thought.

"And number three: We tried to find out who carried Mrs.

Millet's letter to the Pettit. Nobody at the Monarch admits doing that. The limo driver went off duty at eight, and straight home to the bosom of his family. The desk clerk said she left the letter on the counter because Mrs. Millet didn't have a room there. She thought the tour guide might have picked it up?"

Sybil had not seen a letter addressed to Mrs. Millet.

"A man put it through the door," Judy said. "He didn't say much. Just 'Letter for you,' or something like that, and it came tumbling through the slot. I sang out 'Thank you.' That was all there was to it."

"It may not have anything to do with the crime," Chris said, "but it indicates that someone from the Monarch visited the Pettit that night. May I take the letter, Mrs. Millet? We'll check it for fingerprints. I'd like to clear that up."

The letter was still in Margaret's purse, and she handed it over. Very thorough, she thought. And how difficult this particular Scotland Yard Inspector finds his task. He's about out of questions, but can hardly tear himself away. He's fallen head-over-heels for Sybil, just when he most needs his analytical faculties. Might not be a bad match at that. An educated man, by his speech. In Sybil's class, and maybe working at his job for reasons similar to hers. But he doesn't know her—it's just a physical attraction—not like Malcolm, who's had time to know the person behind all that beauty and charm.

Margaret closed her eyes for the merest moment, there on the soft pillows, and when she opened them again Inspector Lamb was gone. Sybil's tawny head was buried in her arms on the table, and Judy patted the cream colored blouse over shoulders that shook with sobs. The sobs must have awakened her. Margaret closed her eyes and lay still. She had interrupted too many times, and this time, Sybil should have her cry, and Judy should comfort her. There was no way to avoid overhearing, however.

"Oh, Mrs. Hark—they're going to check on Richard and find out he was there; I know it! What can I do?" Sybil's voice caught, choked by another overflow.

Sounds of a tissue pulled from the box and Sybil blowing her delicate nose. "Maybe you should tell, or Richard should. As for Inspector Lamb, I'd say he's going to spread his cloak and help you across puddles. Margaret and I will help, too. When the murderer is found, the danger will be over, so don't worry. I think it may be very soon, now. Very soon. You might ask Richard if he delivered that letter—will you do that?"

Chapter 17
Mrs. Hark: Blackmail is Risky

The next morning Inspector Lamb slid into the chair beside Judy Hark who was eating her breakfast in the hotel dining room. He was hollow eyed, rumpled, and unshaven.

"I have bad news," he said. "Very bad news."

Judy arrested her fork in mid air and put it back on her plate. "Bad news? Has something else happened? Are you going to arrest me after all?"

"Yes, yes, and no. Something else has happened, but I'm not going to arrest you, since I was talking to you at the time. Freddie Factor was murdered last night."

Judy looked down at her plate. The tender bacon and the gently cooked egg, oozing a golden drop of yoke where her fork had cut it, suddenly looked revolting. Her stomach churned. "Freddie!" She lifted her eyes to see how Margaret was taking the news.

Margaret was not taking it well. She blurted, "I knew I should have told him! It's all my fault! I should have said..." Her toast went down the wrong way. She coughed and struggled to get her breath, took a sip of water, and finally subsided, red-faced, wheezing, and unable to speak.

Lamb said. "Don't blame yourself, Mrs. Millet. From what you've told me, Factor may have been trying to blackmail a murderer—a risky, foolish thing to do. If anyone else is to blame, I am." His voice was bitter, the voice of a man who had fallen down on his job, whose pride in his work was severely shaken. "I should have noticed him sooner. If I had, I'd have made arrangements with the Bath Police to keep an eye on him, as I did with Goldy Greening and Davis."

A waitress brought a pot of tea. Lamb filled his cup and took a long swallow. "After I left you last night, I did look for him. I called his room and checked around the hotel and the pubs in the neighborhood, but I didn't find him. And I did see Goldy and Davis and the plainclothes man watching them, in the hotel lounge. They were there all evening."

Lamb's chagrin could be heard in his voice, and no wonder. His best suspects had an unshakable alibi. Losing track of Freddie was a serious blunder.

"A patrolman spotted Freddie's body about 11:00 o'clock last night," Lamb said, "in the River Avon, below Pulteney Bridge."

He went on to tell them the Bath Police had called him as soon as they found the hotel key in Freddie's pocket and the tour coupons in his wallet. He'd spent the rest of the night at the police station, phoning Scotland Yard in London and Inspector Nail in Penzance, setting up procedures, and consulting on what to do next. "If I'd had him watched, he would have led us right to the murderer," Lamb groaned.

"Then you think the same party killed him—how was it done?" Judy asked.

"As near as we can tell before the autopsy, he was strangled with his own gold neck chain and dumped over the parapet of the Grand Parade."

Margaret regained her voice. "He didn't know it was the killer! If only I'd warned him!"

"I don't want to frighten you ladies, but this situation is dangerous. We're not making a show because we've got a bus full of potential hostages. I hope if the killer panics, he'll just try to slip away. If he does, we're ready for him with men following the bus and watching at the stops. We'll be in constant communication with headquarters and the police along the route."

Judy was filled with respect. This young officer certainly upheld the reputation of Scotland Yard.

"Now is the time to catch him," Lamb continued. "If he keeps his head and stays with the tour, it's going to be much harder. I want you to watch people. If anyone seems nervous or acts strangely, tell me at once."

Later, Lamb broke the news to the tour group gathered beside the coach. "Ladies and gentlemen, another murder has been done. Mr. Factor, from New York, was killed last night."

The tourists listened in shocked silence as Inspector Lamb outlined the decisions he and his superiors had taken during the night. The group would not be detained as they had been in Penzance. Instead, they would proceed to London with the scheduled stops. That night, they would once again write depositions as to their movements on an evening of murder. After that, most members of the tour could go their own way, but a few would be required to return to Penzance for the inquest on Tony Budge, and possibly to Bath for another inquest, at a time still to be determined.

On Monday, Inspector Lamb would accompany the witnesses to Penzance by train. In Penzance, hotel accommodations were arranged, but not at public expense. They must pay their own way and make any changes in travel plans for themselves.

This speech brought on clamorous protests: "Who has to go to the inquest?" "Change reservations!" "My flight goes tomorrow..." Momentarily abated while Sybil herded them onto the bus, inside the hubbub rose again. "What sort of country is this?" "Tourists murdered—travelers forced into court?" "...at our own expense?" Sybil wisely made no attempt to quell her passengers or to lead morning greetings to their driver. She and Malcolm put their heads together for a moment, then she took her seat next to him, and the bus pulled out into the streets of Bath.

The Americans made the most noise. Chris Lamb sat alone in the seat left vacant by Freddie and Budge, and a large American male, full of pompous self esteem, came up the aisle demanding,

"Who's on the list for this outrage! The wife and I had nothing to do with any murders. Our flight home can't be changed—I've got an important conference in New York the next day. I'll call the American Embassy—you've got no right..."

Judy cringed in shame for her countryman. Lamb asked the man's name, consulted his notebook, and said firmly, "Go back to your seat, Mr. Arnbridge. Try to remember everything you did last night, who saw you do it, and what time. If your deposition checks out, you'll be allowed to go home."

Mr. Arnbridge was the first, but not the last, to hold personal affairs more important than the murder investigation. Lamb refused to name the witnesses or to definitely exclude anyone.

"I'm sure they'll want us to go back to Penzance," Judy said to Margaret.

"I'll be darn disappointed if they don't," Margaret replied. "Hope we can change our London reservations. Thank goodness we have the extra week, or we wouldn't get to see London at all." Their plane tickets were a special tourist rate, nonrefundable, and had to be used on the designated flight two weeks hence.

"You wanted to spend more time in Cornwall, anyway."

"Yes. And I want to see this murderer caught, too. It's a nasty feeling, that we may be traveling with a killer. Poor Freddie! I didn't like him, but he was harmless—he didn't deserve murder. I wonder who else will go back to Penzance?"

"So do I." For miles, Judy watched her fellow passengers. Would the killer try to hijack the bus, as Lamb feared? Surely not. This is no maniac. A heartless opportunist who didn't hesitate to kill, and kill quickly, when his safety was threatened. All he has to do now is be a tourist. Keep on snapping pictures. Keep on seeing the sights. Freddie guessed his identity, but Freddie will never tell.

Judy levered her seat back and tried to relax. They sat near the front of the bus today, with Margaret at the window where she could see the passing countryside, of which she never seemed to tire. Judy closed her eyes and thought about her Willy. What was he doing right now, at home? Had he heard about the murders? She hoped not. It was bad enough in Texas, when she and Margaret helped Crawdad Townley investigate, and Willy was on the spot then, not seven thousand miles away.

And what about Sybil's brother Richard? She must get Sybil alone and find out exactly what he was up to in Penzance. Inspector Lamb still didn't know Richard was there—or did he? He made the connection between Richard and Goldy Greening. Maybe he knew more than she thought.

She reviewed the hotel room session the previous evening, recalling Lamb's acute personal interest in Sybil. He'd have Sybil called for the Penzance inquest, just to have her close by. And Malcolm? Goldy and Davis, almost certainly. Who else?

A gentle mist began to fall as the bus ambled along "roads less traveled" through the Cotswolds, a lovely area of woods and green fields. The bus splashed through small towns bearing such delightfully English names as Cold Ashton, Wooton Bassett, and Lechlade, where houses of Cotswold stone glowed with a honey-colored sheen in the rain.

"The village of Burford is built almost entirely of Cotswold stone," Sybil told them. "Entire hills have been quarried into deep pits to obtain this highly prized building material."

An Englishman across the aisle turned to Judy. "I had a stone cottage in the Cotswolds, once. Very pretty. I nearly died of boredom." He then turned back to his seatmate (presumably his wife) and gave Judy a view of his right shoulder.

At Burford, the lunch stop, the ladies opted for another Devonshire Cream Tea. "We'll never get any more of this after we go home," Margaret said. "I'm not going to let what's happened stop me from enjoying it."

"It does make you think," Judy said, "how easy it must have been to tempt him with something that tastes so good." She added strawberry jam for the perfect flavor combination with scone and cream.

The Quists lunched with them, and Victor said, "We'll miss the Susy Quabble showing if we get tapped for this inquest."

"Oh, no!," Vicky said. "That's the most important one!"

The rain came down harder, pelting their umbrella as they scurried back to the bus.

Judy marveled at Margaret's refusal to let a little thing like two murders spoil her fun. All day, while Judy watched her fellow passengers and mentally composed the deposition she would write when they got to London, Margaret gave every evidence of enjoying her surroundings. At the country churchyard in Bladon, where Churchill was buried, she took pictures of a massive wrought iron gate donated by the Guild of Oxfordshire Smiths and said, "My son-in-law will love this! He's an ironworker himself, you know." In Oxford, the bus dropped them at the portals of Balliol College, and she went into raptures because Balliol was the Alma Mater of Peter Wimsey, Dorothy Sayers' beloved sleuth.

It stopped raining before they reached Hampton Court, a very good thing, as they visited the gardens instead of the interior of Henry VIII's red brick castle. The flowers were lovely and the grass soaking wet, which kept the tourists on the graveled paths.

As usual, Jake Arvin videotaped everything in sight, and Molly trailed along behind him, hung like a pack horse with her purse, an umbrella, and a canvas tote full of video cassettes.

"Are you ladies 'invited' to the inquest?" Molly asked, almost whispering.

"Not so far." Judy said.

"Just because we sat at the same dinner table... you don't think...?" Molly looked anxious and flustered.

Jake heard her and stopped taping. His strange green eyes glared at his wife. "Stop it, Molly. Haven't I told you—it's nothing to do with us—forget it!"

Molly sucked on her cigarette and fluttered her hands among her dangling impedimenta. Her woeful eyes apologized for her husband's bad temper.

"You must be getting some lovely tapes," Judy said hastily. "These gardens are huge!" She waved to the acres of flower beds and orchards of cone-shaped trees planted to form the monogram of William and Mary, Henry's successors at Hampton Court. "Even Hearst Castle doesn't have grounds as large as these."

"We can come back from London and tour the inside. Sybil says there's an excursion boat that comes down the Thames," Margaret chimed in.

The Arvins started off toward the car park, Jake talking to Molly in low, angry tones.

"Well, what do you make of that?"

Margaret shook her head. "I don't know. I hadn't thought Molly was the worrying type."

Back on the road to London, a main highway now, Sybil picked up her microphone. "We are just passing Runnymede," she said. "Runnymede means 'water meadow.' This is the spot where the Barons compelled King John to grant the Magna Carta in 1215. It is considered the birthplace of democracy in England. Of course, the Magna Carta only granted rights to privileged landowners, but it was the first step away from the Divine Right of Kings.

"King John was illiterate, and did not sign the Magna Carta; he sealed the document with his ring.

"Near the Runnymede memorial, there is a monument to John F. Kennedy. The English loved him and deeded this acre of England to the United States in his memory. It is now United States territory."

"Did you know about that?" Judy was much affected by Sybil's words.

"No." Margaret's voice trembled. "Remember when people used to say 'where were you when you heard that Kennedy was shot?'"

She added, "I had a house on Runnymede Street in Canoga

Park, California, right after my divorce. Always thought of that house as a place of liberation."

They reached the Turotel in London without incident. No one hijacked the bus. No one gave the slightest indication of panic, unless you counted Molly Arvin and the others who grumbled over their upset plans.

As the ladies expected, after dinner a policeman brought each of them a summons. Then they labored over their depositions, trying to be accurate even though Chris Lamb had spent most of the fatal evening in their company.

"What time was it when Sybil finally left?" Margaret asked.

"I'm not sure. Didn't we watch the BBC news right afterward? About eleven, I guess."

"Good. She's in the clear, too."

Judy called the Gaddon Hall Hotel in Bloomsbury, where they would have stayed for the coming week, and had no difficulty changing the reservations to the week after. "Thank goodness for that. I was afraid they might be all booked up. Do you realize we have no place to stay tomorrow night? Chris isn't taking the witnesses to Penzance until Monday. Can we stay here, do you think?"

Alarmed, she called the desk—and confirmed her fears. The Turotel was fully booked with new tours coming in on Sunday. No, not a chance. Sorry. When their tours were over, tourists were supposed to go home.

"Call them back at Gaddon Hall and see if we can stay there," Margaret said. "No, wait! Why don't we go to Penzance tomorrow? We don't have to wait for the others, do we? Let's check with Inspector Lamb."

"And call the hotel in Penzance—I don't want to be homeless there, either." Judy enthusiastically fell in with the plan.

"I wonder if Sybil would like to go with us," Margaret said. "If Richard still has his trailer parked near Penzance, maybe we can..."

"Find out about Richard! Oh, yes! I'll call her right now!"

Sybil had also received a summons and agreed that going down to Penzance a day early was a good plan.

The rest of the evening the ladies were busy. Phone calls, train schedules, repacking for Penzance. Margaret decided to leave her large suitcase at Paddington Station and carefully sorted out the clothes she would take for "a week at the beach."

"Take something suitable for the inquest," Judy cautioned.

"And you take your walking shoes. I intend to enjoy the town and the beach and the countryside."

Everything finally arranged, Judy staved off exhaustion long enough to call home. She had no idea what time it was in Gambol Beach, but Willy's comforting voice answered the first ring, as though he had been waiting for her call.

"Willy? How are you, dear? I'm fine. We've changed our plans, and I want you to know how to reach us..." She carefully skirted the murders. Willy showed no signs of knowing about them, so why upset him? There was nothing he could do. Strange, but one country's headline was no news in another. Especially murder in the United States. Coals to Newcastle.

"Call Margaret's family and give them the new schedule, will you, dear?"

Willy promised to pass the word.

Chapter 18
Mrs. Millet: Alias Mystery Writer

Margaret Millet hadn't believed one taxi could handle all three of them and their luggage but the London "black cab" was equal to the job. Tall and old fashioned looking, its roomy rear compartment seated them side by side, with a generous floorboard area for baggage and feet. One stepped up into the taxi and sat high above the road. Margaret felt like the Queen surveying her city as they rolled through London.

Sybil had received a summons too, and must have dreaded the trip to Penzance with the official party. "This is so good of you, Mrs. Hark," she said. "I just couldn't face it. Inspector Lamb—the way he looks at me, watches me... and I must see Richard. Thank you so much for taking me with you."

The cab pushed into Paddington Station and Sybil captured a two-tiered cart for their luggage. No porters. "Oh, no, not in donkey's years," Sybil said. "Unless you have a servant, you push your own trolley these days."

Margaret located the "left luggage" room and read the sign on its tightly closed door: "Sunday hours eleven to five. What a nuisance! After I spent half the night repacking! I'll have to take both bags to Penzance after all."

A round trip to Penzance, second class "saver" fare, cost thirty nine pounds (about seventy dollars). While they waited for the train, Margaret skirted the crowd to photograph wrought-iron scrolls silhouetted against the high arched windows at one end of Paddington Station. Another picture for Tiny, her iron worker son-in-law. She was anxious to talk to Sybil and knew Judy was too, but the bustling station was far too noisy, and there would be plenty of time on the train.

Meanwhile, here she was, Margaret Penfold Millet, actually in London, in Paddington Station, on her way to Cornwall. If only time would stop in this moment! How quickly the first week of the trip went by! Two more weeks and it would be over. She'd be back home, wondering if it all really happened. Please, whoever's winding the clocks—can't we do the next two weeks in slow motion? So I'll have time to absorb it before it's gone?

Nothing stays time or turns out exactly as planned. The chance to talk things over with Sybil, for instance. When the train was called, they trundled the luggage trolley along the tracks, followed by a small, active boy and his plump, chattering mother. They reached a second class car, stowed their baggage on the racks in one end and, after some discussion, chose one of the booth-like seats, Judy and Sybil on one side and Margaret facing them across a formica table.

The small boy bounced gleefully into the next booth, behind Judy and Sybil. His mother cocked her head, listened to their voices, and spoke in clear, strident tones. "Americans, aren't you. Me and Archy likes Americans, don't we Archy? No matter what anybody says! Whistle the Star Banner for the ladies, Archy!"

At any other time, Margaret would have enjoyed meeting an English child and his mother but not now, not when she wanted so much to pump Sybil for information.

Judy asked, "Where are you going today, Archy?"

Archy had no chance to reply, since the question opened his mother's floodgates. "Back to Biddyferd where we lives. I'm a Londoner born and bred, and Archy and me never misses a chance to go up to town and see the sights, do we Archy?" Scarcely taking a breath, she informed them at length that Archy was an after-thought child and she had four other children, three grown up and gone from home. One daughter worked at a small, expensive hotel in the Midlands ("Would you want a good place to stay?") and another worked for the Underground Railway in London, a very fine job.

Judy smiled and nodded, nodded and smiled. She fished a Roosevelt dime out of her purse and handed it to Archy over the seat back. While he examined it minutely, turning the coin over in his pudgy fingers and grating his nails along the milled edge, she turned a quizzical face to Margaret and whispered, "What can we do?"

Margaret tipped the barest suggestion of a wink and nudged Sybil. "You know the mystery I'm writing. I've got this perfectly innocent young man in a trailer in Penzance, and the police are about to find him and accuse him of murder and jewel theft. I have to figure out what he was doing when the victim was killed, and how he got involved with the jewel thieves in the first place!"

"O-o-o-o, a mystery writer!" Archy's mother cried, ears at full extension.

Sybil looked doubtful and for a moment Margaret feared she wouldn't play. Then she smiled her vivid smile. "But the young man wasn't involved in the second jewel theft at all, was he? Maybe he thinks his family jewelry, stolen three years earlier, might be hidden in Penzance. Yes, that's what he's after. The—uh—murder victim knew where these family things were."

"That's good! Oh, Sybil, you're so clever. Let me get out my notebook. Any more ideas?"

"Oh my, that sounds ever so exciting! What's your name, deary? Can I get your book from the library? My name's Nell Archer—that's why we called him Archy—Archy Archer, you know..." Nell had trouble finding a place to stop.

Margaret said "Angela Croft," fervently hoping that wasn't the name of a real author. "Yes, do ask for my books. I hope you enjoy them, Nell. Please excuse us if we work while the train goes along. This is my manager, Mrs. Lamb, and my secretary, Miss Hampton. The new book is called *Poison in Penzance*."

"Yes, please do excuse us," Judy seconded, suppressing a grin and pointedly turning her back on the Archers.

Nell pulled Archy down in their seat and bent over him. "There now, Archy—the ladies has to work, and you must let them be, you hear? She's a writer; how about that? Sh-h-h now—we can listen, can't we." The last was a raspy whisper.

Judy shook with stifled laughter. Margaret didn't dare to meet her eyes. She had pulled their new names out of her darting brain, and now wrote them hastily in her notebook, so as not to forget. Lamb? Of course, Inspector Lamb dominated her thoughts. And they had just visited Hampton Court.

"Isn't there a movie star named Sybil Hampton? Am I famous?" Sybil giggled and her eyes sparkled with mischief.

The train moved slowly at first, then rapidly picked up speed. "Can we get tea on this train? I need it. Shall I see if I can find some? Don't decide any more until I get back." Judy slipped out of the booth and started up the aisle, carefully adjusting her steps to the lurching train.

Sybil's sparkle was short lived. At least she has a sense of humor, Margaret thought, as animation faded from the lovely face. I'll wait 'til Judy comes back with the tea. Judy's so good at getting people to talk about themselves.

She filled the moments by inspecting the train. The English used their trains so casually, in a practical, off-hand way. The luggage rack at the end of the car meant you didn't have to check and claim baggage; you just carried it on, stowed it in the rack, and picked it up on the way out. The car was nearly full and late comers had taken any available seat, with no permission asked from the strangers they joined. The English did that in restaurants, too. If there was a vacant table, they took it, but made no fuss if the only available seats were at tables already occupied. They seemed to have a basic faith in the decency and kindness of those they bumped up against in public places. Of course it might be different in first class—and perhaps in first class restaurants, too. If so, she was glad to be in second.

Margaret gazed out the train window at London clipping by, and mentally reviewed the "case." What Sybil just said had put a new light on Richard's activities; she wanted to hear lots more. Trying to retrieve the family jewels? Was Richard more a product of his rearing than she thought? Maybe he was truly sorry he "blotted his copy book."

Judy returned with cardboard cups of tea and cellophane wrapped cookies labeled "digestive biscuits" in a cardboard tray. The train clattered through the well-groomed Surrey countryside, slowing for the occasional town and then picking up speed.

"Even on trains, they make the tea with boiling water." Judy carefully set the tray on the vibrating table top. "Hope it didn't get too strong on my way back. The lunch counter's five cars up."

Margaret took the lid off her cup, removed the tea bag, and added chemical milk substitute. She opened her notebook and uncapped her ballpoint pen. "Now, then."

Judy picked up the cue. "Yes. Well, let's see—we've got our young man in Penzance. He's hiding out, I should think—wouldn't you say that?"

Sybil chewed a cookie and considered the question. "Yes, definitely. Hiding out from the police, and also from the jewel thieves. You see, he thinks the thieves murdered the man—Pudge? and he's afraid they'll kill him, too, because he knows who they are. Remember that Pudge was the gang's courier. He carried the loot, and the gang leader took the tour to check up on him. She suspected he was selling stones on the side and keeping the money. She also intended to retrieve the jewels Pudge had hidden in or near Penzance three years earlier. Only Pudge knew exactly where."

"She wouldn't carry any of the jewels herself, would she?" Margaret asked.

"Never. She always stayed clear of anything that could incriminate her."

"Yes," Judy said. "She 'keeps clean.' She said that, remember?"

"And it was our young man who 'twigged!'" Margaret responded. Sybil looked mystified, so she recounted what they had overheard at Osbourne House. The best way to receive confidences was to give some.

"Oh, yes, he twigged, all right. He met G... uh, the leader of the gang..."

"Called 'Red.'" Margaret thought of Goldy's flaming hair.

"Yes. He met Red through some of his raffish friends several years ago. She was very cautious, but hinted she could put him in the way of a sizeable bit of money—a thousand pounds, no less. All he had to do was give a friend of hers a floor plan of our—this manor house—with the location of the safe marked and leave a side door unlocked at the right time. The jewels were well insured. They were also entailed—they couldn't be sold."

"How is that? I don't understand," Judy said.

"It's something they do here," Margaret explained. "When an estate is entailed, it can only pass to another member of the family; it can't be sold on the open market. The heir inherits, but doesn't really own, the property. It belongs to the family and to future heirs."

"Exactly. You do understand us. The land was entailed too, but Fa—his father—was able to break the entail after the fire. He mortgaged the land heavily to rebuild the manor house, and when he couldn't pay back, the lenders sued for it and won."

"So, in a way, our young man was only trying to liberate some cash—for his family as well as himself. They would get the insurance money, he thought. Dishonest, but still..."

Margaret finished her tea and looked across at Nell and little Archy. Archy had lost interest. His mother gave him a lurid comic book from her tote bag, moved him to her other side, and slid to a better listening position. She had not lost interest at all. She was obviously fascinated and intended to miss nothing.

"Perhaps that's enough for now. Let me organize my notes and see what comes next." Margaret bent to her notebook. Sybil blinked and stared out the window. Judy gathered up the litter from their tea and sought a trash container. Nell bore her disappointment and allowed Archy to read some of the adventures of Snakeman to her from his comic book.

"Bid uh ferd, next stop Bid uh ferd..."

Archy and Nell scrambled to collect their belongings, by now scattered on seat, table, and floor. "Our stop—what a treat to meet you ladies—pick up your paper, Archy—where's your cap—goodbye—goodbye—I'll read your book..."

And they were gone. As the train pulled out of Bideford, three young hikers piled their knapsacks in the baggage section, claimed the empty booth and began to chatter among themselves. The two boys eyed Sybil appreciatively but saw she was well chaperoned and let it go. They hadn't the slightest interest in old ladies, not even American ones.

Margaret enjoyed the train ride through the green English countryside and for her, the best sight of the entire trip greeted them at the Penzance Station: Malcolm, roving the platform, his thick dark hair ruffled in the breeze, his warm brown eyes searching the carriage windows for—Sybil's face. His joyous smile when he saw her stirred Margaret's normally unsentimental heart.

Chapter 19
Mrs. Hark: Steak and Kidney Pie

Malcolm's jeans, jersey pullover and canvas jogging shoes were such a change from his driver's uniform that at first Judy Hark didn't recognize him. "How on earth did you get here?" she asked, as he shifted their baggage out of the train.

Malcolm took his eyes off Sybil long enough to answer, "In my trusty MG. It won't carry all this, though. I'll get you a cab." He grabbed a nearby trolley and piled on the bags, all but Sybil's carryall, which she had picked up.

Sybil hadn't said a word, but looked terribly pleased. She asked Malcolm, "Were you summoned, too?"

"Well, not exactly. No, as a matter of fact. I had a spot of leave coming; just decided to come on down."

Malcolm was saved further explanations by the business of engaging a taxi and loading luggage, Judy, and Margaret Millet (in that order) into it. Judy told the driver, "Bond Hotel," and Malcolm led Sybil toward an ancient, yellow MG roadster parked nearby. He was limping, and she wondered why. "Can you believe it? Right out from under our noses."

Margaret chuckled. "Ain't no flies on our boy Malcolm. A damsel in distress—to the rescue! He must have come flying in that little car, to beat the train."

Rooms were reserved for the witnesses at the Bond Hotel on Church Street; a humble hostelry compared to the splendid Monarch, but ancient and steeped in Cornish history. Its original stone walls could be seen in the lower corridors, inside now due to additions. The large dining room had seen the ball where Nelson's great victory and sad death at Trafalgar were first announced, in 1805.

Judy learned these things from a folder she picked up at the desk. While Margaret surveyed the view from their room (gray rooftops running downhill to Penzance Harbor), she read aloud, "In its long history, the Bond has provided accommodation for Royalty, Prime Ministers and great artistes. All travelers have been assured of a good meal, a hot bath, and a comfortable bed."

"What shall we have first?" Margaret asked.

"I want all those things, but what I need even more is exercise. All this sitting on buses and trains..."

"I know what you mean. Let's walk to the waterfront. We can come back and bathe before dinner."

"And find Sybil again, I hope." Judy slipped out of her pumps and into a pair of soft leather walkers.

On the sea front, the air was glorious—warm, salty, clean, with a gentle Southwest breeze. Puffy white clouds passed rapidly across a baby-blue sky, suggesting a stronger wind aloft. The four o'clock sun slanted down, lighting both the Esplanade and the deep water at its edge, where a high speed motorboat race was in progress.

"Look! He just missed the other boat!" Judy and Margaret joined the wandering crowd that watched the race. The smell of hot sausage-in-a-bun stopped them at a vendor's cart. "Oh, let's! I'm so hungry."

"Spoil our appetites for dinner, I expect. Good, though, aren't they?" Judy took another mustardy bite. Sparkling with white paint, a metal post-and-cable fence kept careless strollers from dropping a dozen feet into the deep water below.

The race ended and the boats idled toward the sea wall, where a ledge and stairs made it possible to disembark.

In just those few minutes some of the fluffy clouds had consolidated into a dark mass and warm rain began to pelt the promenaders. They scuttled to a half open shelter, well dampened on the way. Huddled under the roof, they watched the downpour bounce off the red block paving, rapidly forming puddles and streams that ran into the sea. The shower passed, and steam rose from the puddles in little puffs.

"Wet!" Judy said, and they were. Margaret's tennis shoes squelched all the way back to the hotel. The sun came out like a sweet apology, which they laughed and accepted.

"Room 19," Judy said at the desk, brushing drops of water off her shoulders. "We got caught in the rain!"

The clerk, a dark, pleasant woman of generous proportions, pulled their key from its cubbyhole along with a folded bit of paper. "Message for you," she said. An enormous, black Persian cat, crouching on the counter, picked that moment to rise under the clerk's hand. The key clattered to the floor and the note sailed away, landing gracefully in a potted palm. The clerk laughed. "Meet Poldark." She petted the cat's silky ears. He arched his back and stretched, then turned his golden eyes to Judy and raised one paw to command her attention.

Margaret retrieved note and key. "Poldark," she said. "A Cornish cat, then."

"As Cornish as they come. He's the owner's cat, but thinks he's the real owner. Head Greeter, you know. I'm Mrs. Canady. From Somerset, but he tolerates me. He's named for the chap in the books—have you read them?—the books about Poldark."

Margaret stroked Poldark, to his obvious satisfaction, and Judy chatted with Mrs. Canady, who had been to California and declared that Santa Monica was a lovely place, but "not like Penzance, is it?"

"Have any of the other witnesses come today?" Judy asked.

"Witnesses? Is that it, then! We did wonder why Chief Inspector Nail made all these reservations. Is it the American chap who was killed up at the Pettit?"

"Yes, the inquest on Tuesday."

"Well, you two and Miss Darington—you called last night, didn't you. We expect the others tomorrow. Inspector Lamb—is it true he's from Scotland Yard? And two singles, two doubles—they didn't give us the names—for Monday, Tuesday and Wednesday." Mrs. Canady studied her room chart.

"I see. And you know that Mrs. Millet and I will stay all week; we're on vacation."

They climbed the carpeted stairs, admiring the glossy mahogany railing and a huge linen chest of carved teak wood on the landing. A three-tiered table and a low-backed chair stood in the hall just outside their room. Judy said, "What lovely antiques. Better than anything in the shops at home."

"And they've probably been in use here ever since they were new," Margaret answered. "I'll flip you for first bath. Gosh, I've got to get these wet shoes off. Only tennies I brought, too. Hope I can get them dry before we take any hikes."

Inside the room, Margaret read the note. "From Sybil. 'I'm in room #23. Malcolm is taking me out to see Richard. Can you meet us for dinner? Eight o'clock? We'll wait for you at the Smuggler's Inn.'"

"The Smuggler's Inn—where's that?"

"Malcolm's favorite place. He took me there the night..."

"I wonder if Richard will come too?"

"I do hope so," Margaret went into the bathroom. "Oh, bother. No wash cloths." Water poured noisily into the bathtub.

When Judy saw the spotlighted "smuggler" figure with one leg over the ridge of the inn's roof and a knife in its toothy grin, she said, "Crime isn't new in Cornwall, is it?"

"I don't think smuggling was considered a crime," Margaret said. "It was just a way to avoid taxes. Look, here's Sybil."

They were punctual, and Sybil watched for them. "There you are. Thanks for coming. The others are downstairs." She led the way down the steep stairs, along a narrow aisle to a private booth and helped Judy out of her flowered jacket. "Sit by Richard, Mrs. Hark. Richard, these are the friends I told you about; Mrs. Millet and Mrs. Hark." Malcolm slid to the back of the booth and Margaret scooted in beside him, leaving room for Sybil on the outside.

A stoutish woman with a long white apron brought menus. "Mr. Trewbridge, how nice to see you. And you've brought us more customers, haven't you? Would you like a whole pie? Just out of the oven."

"That I would, Mrs. Phillips—if agreeable to all. Steak and kidney pie?" Malcolm looked around the booth for assent. "Yes, then, that's settled. What will you have to drink, ladies?"

"I'll have a half of lager," Judy said, as Margaret had taught her. What a good host Malcolm Trewbridge makes, she thought. How strange that I've never heard his last name before. Trewbridge—remember that. She exchanged a look with Margaret, who nodded and moved her lips, "Trewbridge."

"Have you tried our Cornish cider?" Mrs. Phillips asked.

It seemed cider was the proper accompaniment for steak and kidney pie. Malcolm warned, "It's potent, Cornish cider. Goes down easy, kicks you later."

"I'll be careful. Yes, I'd like to try some cider."

Richard ordered a bottle of Burgundy. "Cider doesn't agree with me, I'm afraid." He was roughly clad in jeans and a heavy wool sweater, like a disguise on his lithe form. A racehorse harnessed to the plow, Judy mused, catching his finely drawn profile from the corner of her eye.

A fat candle in a glass bowl lit the booth dimly. She turned against the high back of the heavy wooden seat for a better view of her companions. Malcolm had changed his jeans and jersey for slacks, tweed sport coat, crisp white shirt and well chosen tie. He was a fine looking man, with his thick dark hair and warm brown eyes. Richard was more than handsome; he was beautiful, like his sister. A slender, English version of the blond Apollo.

Mrs. Phillips placed a steaming pie in the middle of the table. She plunged a serving spoon through the golden crust, left it upright in the pie, and dealt thick, warm plates to each diner. Malcolm did the honors, passing generous servings around the table. Mrs. Phillips brought a bowl of stewed plums, said, "Enjoy your food," and departed.

Judy tried the steak and kidney pie. "It's wonderful. I've never tasted anything like it. Tell me, Richard, do you cook for yourself in your trailer?"

"Not really. Mostly take-away," Richard mumbled.

"He's awful," Sybil said, "takes no care of himself at all. I'm glad he's getting a good meal."

Judy ate with pleasure and sampled the Cornish cider with care. It was potent indeed, and she left her glass two-thirds full, sipping from a tumbler of water instead. Richard, she noticed, made heavy inroads on his bottle of Burgundy, and by the end of the meal, his finely chiseled lips had loosened and he stared defiantly across the table at his sister.

"I suppose you're waiting for me to tell all," he said, "but for the life of me, I can't see the use of it. What earthly good can these people do? It's an added risk, just coming out in public. Don't know why I let you talk me into it."

"But you must let us help you, Richard. Who else is there? You can't lurk in that caravan forever. The police will find you." Sybil's voice shook with concern.

"That's right," Malcolm said. "We're here to help."

Margaret whispered, "We can't help you unless we know what happened. Why don't you just tell us exactly what you did and saw the night Budge was murdered." The others bent closer and strained to hear.

It was contagious; Judy whispered, too. "Yes. Just tell us, Richard, and don't leave out a thing."

The candle flickered and glinted in Richard's eyes. "Very well," he said, without bothering to lower his voice. "If you will have it."

He filled his wine glass for the fifth time. "It didn't start with Budge's murder. It started with Goldy Greening. I met her at a party in town—in London. People have sort of taken her up; she's invited everywhere. Good amusement value, you know, with her diamonds and her bodyguard and all that. Besides, she's rolling, and generous—never seems to mind a touch.

"I was hard up at the time, and she—well, to get to the point, she offered to put me in the way of a sizeable bit of the ready. I'd been moaning about how all our assets were tied up in land and jewelry, et cetera, and she put me wise to a party who specialized, she said, in breaking entails for people like us. The jewels politely lifted, the insurance people fork over the cash, Simple Simon.

"Simple—what a laugh. Father was to get the insurance, I'd get a thousand pounds for cooperating, and the crooks would get the jewels. The crooks got the jewels, all right, but it seems they mislaid them. The police laddies found the neat little floor plan I'd drawn, right under the safe. What a bloody great blow-up we had then!"

"Sybil told us," Judy said. "Did you get the thousand pounds?"

"No. It was payment on delivery, and the goods were never delivered. That's why, when I saw Goldy Greening's name on Sybil's roster for this little jaunt, I decided to tag along. After all, it wasn't my fault the stuff had gone missing. I thought maybe she'd pay up."

"We saw you with her in the Portsmouth Pub," Margaret put in. "What did she have to say?"

"Quite a lot. She was on the tour to watch Budge, the courier for the gang. Seems she thought he might be getting greedy. He told her he'd buried the loot from our robbery because the police got too close. He'd received it all right, hand delivered in Penzance—but he was afraid to carry it out of the country and said he cached it for later. Budge was too smart to tell her where he hid the stuff; he wanted to be needed, you see."

"And why did she tell you all this?" Judy asked.

"She wanted me to help her watch Budge. What she didn't tell me was that they planned to burgle the Cromarth Collection and give him another package to carry. If I've got it straight, she was playing business as usual with Budge and planning to fire him, permanently, as soon as he picked up what was hidden. And it looks like she did."

Judy didn't tell him that Goldy and Davis had an iron-clad alibi for the second murder, that of Freddie Factor. Inspector Lamb, that shining light of Scotland Yard, could be wrong about both crimes being the work of one murderer. "What was your plan, Richard? You were going to 'fix everything,' you told Sybil. How was that?"

Richard shot Sybil a furious glance and raised his wine glass for a long swallow. "It could have worked. Budge couldn't call the police, could he? The tour only had one night in Penzance, and if our jewels were here, he'd have to pick them up, wouldn't he? I was going to rob the robber, that's all, and sell the stuff in Amsterdam myself. But he was dead when I got there. Goldy beat me to him. God, he was a mess."

Malcolm, who had listened carefully, now spoke. "And Goldy knows you can pull her right in! Me lad, you'd be safer in jail."

"Oh, that's true, Richard. Please," Sybil pleaded. "Please talk to Inspector Lamb and tell him everything. It's the only way!"

Margaret wore what Judy thought of as her inscrutable face. "What if Goldy didn't kill Budge, and thinks you did, Richard? What if she thinks you have all the jewels both sets?"

Chapter 20
Mrs. Millet: Wash Cloths and Witnesses

Sybil stayed at The Smuggler, trying to persuade Richard to talk to the police, while Malcolm walked the ladies back to the Bond Hotel. He still hobbled and Margaret asked, "Why are you limping, Malcolm? Did you hurt yourself?"

"It's my footer knee. Much as I love my MG, I pay when I drive it very far. It's the feet-straight-out-in-front position, I guess."

"Football?" Judy asked. "I didn't know the English played football."

"No, rugby."

He left them at the door to their room with, "I'm up another flight, where it's cheaper. Have to share the bath, but beggars can't be choosers, can we?"

The next morning, Margaret woke early and mulled over the night before. Malcolm, spending his own money to be in Penzance for Sybil. Malcolm at the Smuggler's Inn, where his quiet, sympathetic presence added something for everyone—strength for Sybil, control for Richard, comfort for her and Judy. I hope—oh, how I hope—that Richard listened to his sister and will talk to Inspector Lamb, she thought. I've never suffered fools gladly, and hearing his story... well, Richard is a fool. Rob the robbers! Did he think a gang of jewel thieves would let him get away with that? Preposterous!

Mostly, she was amazed at her own change of heart. She had held back, dragging her feet, wanting to stay out of trouble—and now she wanted so much to understand and do something! When did that happen? Perhaps when Budge's satchel turned up in Judy's suitcase. And there were Sybil and Richard, living examples of her pet theory about extremely beautiful people. She'd always thought they were different and led different lives. People either adored or despised them, and seldom went past their appearance to the human being inside. And in Sybil's case, there was a real human being inside. Richard, now—but she was thinking in circles.

The thing is, I'll never be at peace again until these crimes are solved and the murderer caught. Judy—I must talk it all over with Judy, thoroughly, before Inspector Lamb and the other witnesses get here.

Judy was still asleep and needed the rest, so she wrote in her journal and waited.

Judy woke late—too late to do anything but dress quickly and go down to breakfast before the dining room stopped serving.

Not only that, she had her own agenda for the day. She took a slice of crunchy toast from the silver rack and said, "There are things we need to do. Find a laundromat, for one. We'll ask Mrs. Canady. I need film; maybe we can get our pictures developed, too, since we'll be here all week. And let's try to get a street map. It's always easier to find your way around if you have a map."

Margaret said, "We can buy tea and munchies to have in our room. No need to eat restaurant food all the time." It was more than the money. She fed very simply at home and rich restaurant food often disagreed with her.

So they spent the morning on creature needs. In bright sunshine and fresh breezes, they lugged suitcases full of dirty clothes uphill to the "Washateria" on the street called Causeway Head. While the machines worked, they browsed the nearby shops. A newsstand took their film to be developed, provided a free Penzance street map, and sold them a copy of the *Western Morning News*, "The Voice of Cornwall. All the local and national news you need," according to the masthead.

"I see it's printed in Plymouth—isn't that in Devon?" Judy asked.

At a store displaying toiletries in the window, Margaret clapped hand to forehead and exclaimed, "Of course! Sponges! That's why no wash cloths in the hotel rooms, Judy—the English carry their own sponges in sponge bags. Mentioned in all the books—Dornford Yates put a sponge-bag in every story he ever wrote. I should have remembered!"

"Really? Well, I don't want to carry a wet sponge around. Maybe we can buy wash cloths here."

They went in, but found no wash cloths. The clerk said, "If it's face cloths you mean, there's a shop down the hill that carries nature stuff. I think they have some there."

The recommended shop was called "Remedies" and carried only organic, natural goods. Inside, it smelled of pot pourri and vanilla candles, alight behind the counter. A basket of small, flimsy wash cloths was prominently displayed, and soaps, lotions, and beauty preparations of all kinds filled the shelves.

Margaret fingered a wash cloth. "Not very substantial."

"But light enough to dry easily. I'll take two," Judy said.

"So will I." Margaret also bought bubble bath and henna shampoo, planning a luxuriant soak and head washing later in the day.

At noon, they carried suitcases full of clean, dry, neatly folded garments back to the Bond Hotel. A window caught Margaret's eye and she lagged behind to look in. A motto inscribed in gilt letters on a white plaque had pride of place. GOOD COURAGE BREAKS ILL LUCK. Behind the window, the dim shop was stuffed with old books and assorted treasures. She noted the location for future reference.

Judy had stopped half a block away. She laughed and said, "A bookstore, I might have known. Do you want to go in?"

"Later. Let's buy some food and go back to the room. We need to talk before Inspector Lamb shows up."

Penzance didn't run to supermarkets; food was sold in individual, specialized shops. They visited a fruit stand, a bakery and a purveyor of teas and cheeses.

When they reached the hotel the ladies were so burdened they could barely manage the stairway. Margaret left her suitcase on the landing to lighten her load, deposited her parcels in the room, and then went back for the bag. She noticed again the fine carving of the antique linen chest. The rich, dark wood looked as though it had been polished every week of its long life.

"Home again," Judy sighed. "How about a cup of tea?" Cups and saucers for two and an electric kettle came with the room. When she filled the kettle, the corroded heating element flaked off into the water. "Here, this isn't very nice." Even after she scrubbed it, the kettle imparted a metallic taste to the Oolong Tea, but they drank it, ate fruit and cheese and buns, and felt refreshed.

"Now," Margaret said, "Let's put our heads together. Remember how we wrote down all we knew, that time in Texas? Didn't it help? Let's do it again."

This time she had no supply of lined yellow paper, but her spiral notebook was blank except for the scribbles made on the train. "First, let's consider the possibilities. What do you think really happened?"

"I still think Freddie had the best chance to put that satchel in my suitcase. And why did he refuse to look for Budge when Sybil asked him to? He could have killed Budge—and then the gang killed Freddie."

"Okay, we'll put that down as possibility number one." Margaret wrote in the notebook. "If true, there's at least one unknown member of the gang, who killed Freddie and may or may not be a member of the tour, because Goldy and Davis were being watched by the police when that happened.

"Possibility number two; the gang killed both Budge and Freddie, and tried to confuse the issue with Budge's satchel."

"You'd think," Judy said, "they'd try to call attention to Richard, not me. He was their 'fall guy' before. Could that be why Goldy told him to watch Budge? To draw him in?"

"Could be. And would the gang kill Budge before he retrieved the Darington jewels? I don't think he had time to do that, do you? That makes number two look unlikely." She noted the discrepancies.

Judy said, "However unpleasant, I think we have to list possibility number three: Richard killed both Budge and Freddie."

Margaret listed it. "Several questions on that one. Why is he still here? Because he didn't get the Darington jewels—maybe. But I think he'd have bolted. And would Freddie have recognized him, fooling with your suitcase?"

"Did Richard go to Bath? Maybe we can find out. He may have a solid alibi for Freddie's murder."

"We must check." Margaret wrote rapidly. "And number four will be the toughest to solve, but fits the best, I think. Budge was killed by someone he knew and let into his room, someone on the tour, someone Freddie recognized in the hall, the next morning. And when Freddie tried to blackmail him or her, Freddie was killed without hesitation. That took strength and/or skill. I'm betting on a man, but a woman is possible, especially if she was into physical fitness and self-defense training. Vicky Quist could have done it, for instance."

"A lot of people could have done it." Judy shook her head. "What do we know about any of these people, really? If it's number four, it must have been done for the Cromarth Collection alone. The murderer wouldn't even know about the Darington jewels, would he?"

"From what the newspaper said, the Cromarth Collection is plenty of motive," Margaret said. "And Inspector Lamb is right; if the murderer plays it cool and keeps on being a normal tourist, he or she is going to be hard to catch. Unless he or she still has the jewels. Where would you keep a packet of jewels so the police couldn't find them, Judy?"

"I don't know, but I'll think about it."

Margaret and Judy did not meet the train from London, but they casually loitered in the hotel lobby at the appropriate time.

Grunt Davis held the heavy door while Goldy sailed in, trailing her fox stole over a fluttering costume in emerald green. Blocking the door open with his large foot, Davis bumbled several pieces of luggage through it and followed Goldy to the desk.

"What kind of a dump is this? Why aren't we staying at the Monarch?" Goldy demanded, inspecting her surroundings with scorn.

Mrs. Canady fixed her with a frosty eye and said, "Your name, Madame?"

Margaret, as always, found Goldy fascinating and it took a nudge from Judy to call her attention to the others who now entered. Her lips formed a silent whistle. Our own little subgroup of the tour; Jake Arvin, his weird green eyes hidden by yellow sunglasses, Molly puffing her cigarette and that inseparable duo, Victor and Vicky Quist, in their khaki travelers' vests. Why? What did Inspector Lamb learn about these people to set them apart from the other tourists? She shook her head and resolved to find out.

Chief Inspector Nail rose from a lounge chair behind the potted palm and came forward to greet the witnesses. His cold, assessing eyes passed over her and Margaret shuddered, as from an icy wind. This is not a game, she thought. It's murder. The answer to the puzzle, if I find it, could make me a prime candidate for "third victim" of a calculating, greedy killer. Is that killer here, in the lobby of the Bond Hotel?

Chapter 21
Mrs. Hark: The Ransacked Room

Judy Hark also wanted to know why these witnesses were chosen. Before the ladies withdrew to their own room, she had a few words with Inspector Lamb, who looked hollow eyed and exhausted.

"We're in Room 19. Can you stop by after dinner?"

"Where's Syb—Miss Darington?"

"She'll be with us. About nine o'clock?"

Lamb nodded and Judy passed on. She had no idea whether Sybil would be with them or not, but if that was what it took to get Lamb's attendance, she would try to arrange it.

Judy rested, showered, and dressed for dinner.

Margaret put on her jacket and went out, returning later with a flat package wrapped in brown paper and string, and a grubby little book. Judy remembered the book store they had passed that morning and smiled. If this kept up, Margaret would have to throw away her clothes to make room for books in her suitcase. What had she bought now? The book, she could see, was The Happy Prisoner, by Monica Dickens. "What's in the package?"

"Something for Sybil. Have you called her?"

"I left a message at the desk. I left word for Malcolm, too, asking him to call us tonight." Judy cast a disapproving eye on her friend. "Is that what you're wearing to dinner?" She herself wore a peach colored frock of soft, crushed cotton with a full skirt. A long rope of amber and carved wooden beads reflected the sparkle of her intricate, dangling earrings. She did wish Margaret would dress up once in a while. Really, that navy blue pants suit...

"Well, I did bring both suitcases. Do I have time to change?"

"Take time."

Margaret laughed, but did as she was bid, donning white slacks and a royal blue silk shirt.

"Now that's your color. Put on your rainbow earrings, and I'll take you to dinner."

As promised in the brochure, the hotel dining room was big enough for a full dress ball. Historic it might be, but it was also old. Rows of square pillars supported the high ceiling, and the uncarpeted wooden floor creaked ominously underfoot. A large portrait hung just inside the entrance arch; Admiral Lord Nelson, with a background of sailing ships in flaming combat. A serving table crowded with water pitchers stood beneath the painting. Judy suppressed a flighty giggle; were the pitchers of water there to dowse the blazing ships?

On a Monday this late in the season, diners were few. The only sound was the hurried, echoing tread of a waitress with hard-soled shoes. Dark shadows obscured the farther end of the room, its chandeliers unlit. Only a few of the widely spaced tables bore white linen covers and cockaded orange napkins. The Arvins and the Quists shared one, and Christopher Lamb sat near a tall window, dining with Chief Inspector Nail. Goldy Greening and Davis were not there, nor were Sybil and Malcolm.

"Two, please," Judy told the waitress. They followed her black-taffeta back to a small table overlooking the harbor lights. She gave them shabby, end-of-the-season menus, then rushed back for a pitcher to fill their water glasses. She was the only hotel employee in sight.

Margaret said, "I'll have the seafood platter."

The waitress looked doubtful. "I'm not sure we have that tonight, Madam; I'll have to check."

"What do you have for sure?" Judy asked.

"The roast beef, the lamb stew..."

"I'll have roast beef."

"If you don't have the seafood, I'll have roast beef, too." Margaret sighed. The waitress pulled a pad from the pocket of her starchy white apron, jotted their order, and swished away.

Margaret said, "Do you know, I still haven't checked the telephone book for Penfolds? I must do that, first thing tomorrow."

"Where do you suppose Sybil and Malcolm are?" Judy's mind was on more urgent matters. "And Goldy and Grunt? Are the police watching them, do you think?"

"Goldy's probably dining at the Monarch. Historical places like this wouldn't impress her." Margaret looked out over the dark rooftops of Penzance to the necklace of street lights, haloed in fog, around the harbor.

"I wish the inquest could be the end of it," Judy said. "I wish they'd figure out who killed Budge and Freddie and settle it, then and there. I don't mind telling you, Margaret, I'm scared."

"You? Scared?" Margaret pooh-poohed that idea. "The inquest will be 'continued' for lack of evidence—I think that's the word. If only the jewels could be found and connected to the killer!"

Yes, Judy reflected, that's the key to the whole business. The jewels must be found. What are the police doing about it? She must persuade Inspector Lamb to tell them, later that night.

Roast beef arrived on steaming platters, accompanied by brussels sprouts and slices of rich Yorkshire pudding. Nothing further was said about seafood. The English should all be big as barns, Judy thought, if they eat like this every night—especially since they have that extra meal called 'tea' in the afternoon.

From her chair, she could see through the dining room entrance to the hallway and staircase beyond. Suddenly, her eye was caught by a dark figure, rapidly climbing the stairs. A large woman, enveloped in a baggy coat and head scarf, carrying a shopping bag. She looked like a housekeeper or cleaning woman; why was she using the main stairway? For a woman that size, she was certainly nimble. In a hurry, too. The figure climbed out of view and Judy turned back to her loaded plate.

The Arvins and the Quists departed. The Quists wore invisible robes of innocence as they stopped at the ladies' table to grumble about their spoiled plans. "Surely, they'll let us go after the inquest," Vicky said plaintively. "Just because we ate at the same table—well, I guess they had to have somebody testify."

Victor said, "What a nuisance! We need to get back to London." They both looked at Judy with suspicion, as though she and Margaret were there for guiltier reasons.

Jake Arvin said, "Sorry you ladies got mixed up in this. It'd be too bad if something happened to you. Be careful. My advice is stay in your room until the inquest and then leave Penzance as fast as you can." He spoke in a flat, even tone that made Judy shiver, his green eyes half closed, his face an expressionless mask. "Come on, Molly. Let's go." He took his wife's arm. Molly held back, wanting to speak, then gave it up and allowed Jake to march her away.

Punctually at nine o'clock, Inspector Lamb tapped on the door of room 19. Judy let him in. He looked eagerly for Sybil, and his face sagged in disappointment when he didn't see her.

"Is it important, Mrs. Hark? I'm out on my feet. Sleep's been hard to come by these last few days."

"Come in, Inspector. Sybil will be along. Do sit down."

Margaret rose from the only chair and moved to sit on the nearest bed. "Grapes? They're right beside you."

Judy said, "Sybil will have things to tell you, Inspector. You do look tired. I expect you've worked very hard to check on everybody and decide who should come to the inquest."

"Why the Arvins and the Quists, is it?" Lamb dropped into

the chair and pulled a stem of green grapes from the bunch. He popped one into his mouth and gulped as the juice burst down his throat. "Well, I don't mind telling you. Jake Arvin offered us some video tapes—shots filmed while Budge and Factor were still alive. One in particular..."

Margaret perked up. "Was it taped at Osborne House, on the Isle of Wight?"

"How did you know?"

Judy remembered the incident. "We're in it too, I bet. Budge was hiding from the camera, wasn't he? We thought it was strange at the time."

Lamb nodded. "And as for the Quists..." He hesitated, and seemed to consider whether or not to go on.

"Yes?"

"Their dress shop in Virginia... well, our sources tell us there's a case in the back of the store where they show antique jewelry. Nothing very remarkable on display, but the word is that more valuable pieces are sometimes shown to special customers."

Margaret gasped. "They never said a word to us about jewelry, did they Judy? That is intriguing, isn't it!"

"They mentioned costume jewelry to me," Judy said. "Vicky says no outfit is complete without the right accessories. It's worth investigating, I suppose, but it may not mean anything."

Margaret refused to be dampened, and seemed about to review the entire matter in light of this new idea. Judy cut her off. "What can be keeping Sybil? I'll just try her room again."

As she touched the telephone, it jingled under her hand. "There. Is that you, Sybil?"

"Mrs. Hark? Thank God, are you all right? Oh, my room! Someone's torn it apart! Wreckage! We just got back—what shall I do?" Sybil's voice rose to the edge of hysteria.

"Stay put. Inspector Lamb is here—we'll be right with you." Judy dropped the receiver and dashed to the door. "Sybil's room's been trashed—come on!"

Three doors down the hall, Malcolm and Richard stood in the

doorway and Sybil, her frightened face turned toward them, in the middle of a prodigious mess, the telephone still in her hand. Drawers were pulled out, their contents scattered. Suitcases looked as if they had exploded. The mattress was tumbled off the bed, slit on the sides, handfuls of stuffing everywhere. The wardrobe gaped. In the bathroom, the top of the toilet tank lay in three pieces on the floor.

"So destructive," Margaret murmured.

"Vicious," Judy said. "Not just looking for something; meant to frighten."

Inspector Lamb pushed past them. "Please step outside, Miss Darington. I'll want a crime team to go over this. It may be connected with the case."

"Come to our room, dear." Judy took Sybil's hand and patted it gently. "I'll make you a cup of tea." Tea, the English comforter, she thought. I'm learning local customs.

The six of them trooped down the hall to room 19, where Chris Lamb called the Penzance police station and Judy "brewed up." Sybil was ensconced in the chair. Richard plopped on the floor beside her, as though his legs would no longer hold him up. Malcolm sat beside Margaret on one of the beds, running his hands nervously through his thick, dark hair, already a wild tangle.

Judy, with only two cups, gave one to Sybil and the other to Richard, the two who seemed to need it most. If Sybil looked frightened, Richard looked terrified. He took the scalding cup of tea with hands shaking so hard he could scarcely hold it.

Lamb put down the telephone. "Now then, Sybil," he said. (What happened to 'Miss Darington'? Judy thought.) "Please tell me everything you can. This isn't a hotel burglary—someone was looking for something, most likely the stolen jewels. Why would they look in your room?"

Sybil eyed Richard and said, "I haven't the least idea."

"That won't do, Sybil. These people mean business. If they think you have the jewels or know where they are, you are in danger—serious danger." Lamb's voice was personal, tender with meaning. He cared. The two of them might have been alone in the room. Malcolm gave his hair a desperate tug and turned to Margaret, his face like that of a slapped child.

Richard looked up, stuttered a bit, and blurted, "I want you to put me in jail!"

"Why, Darington? What have you done?"

"N-n-nothing. It's me they're after, not Sybil. It's the g-gang—Goldy Greening and friends. They stole the Cromarth collection. Just lock me up where they can't get at me, and I'll be your witness. I'll tell you the whole thing."

"And the Darington robbery? Is that included in the deal?"

"Why not? Can you protect me? Lock up the lot of them, can't you?"

"That requires evidence, not wild accusations."

Lamb cocked his head, then opened the door to the hall. Judy heard sounds of heavily-shod feet on the stairs. The Penzance Police had arrived.

"Chief Inspector," Lamb called. "Here's a witness for you. Take him in like a good chap, and let me find myself a bed."

Chapter 22
Mrs. Millet: Inquest Adjourned

"Yes, I've got to find a bed." Inspector Lamb turned to Sybil. "And so do you." Sybil had kissed her brother and sent him bravely off to the police station. "It'll be hours before the crime team is finished with your room, and I'm not sure you'd be safe there when they are."

"We can see to that, Inspector," Margaret said. "You go on. You look like you could drop into a coma any minute."

"That's right. We can look after Sybil." Malcolm added his backing.

Lamb gazed Svengali-like into Sybil's eyes. "Don't tell anyone where you are... wait for me."

Sybil backed stiffly away, touching shoulders with Malcolm. "I'll be fine, Inspector. Don't give it another thought."

The action and reaction among the three of them would have been funny under other circumstances, Margaret thought. When Lamb walked away, she sighed with relief. "Well, that's over. Sybil, I have something for you, and I can't think of a more appropriate time. Your room an uninhabitable mess, and your brother off to jail—if ever anybody needed this, it's you." She handed Sybil the small brown-paper parcel she'd acquired before dinner. "Go ahead, open it."

Sybil loosened the string and unwrapped the small white plaque, with Malcolm looking over her shoulder. "GOOD COURAGE BREAKS ILL LUCK," Malcolm read, and Sybil let out a shaky peal of laughter.

"Oh, Mrs. Millet, you would give Good Courage to a rabbit. Thank you, I shall treasure it."

Judy picked up the phone. "Let's call the desk and see if they can give you another room." After her call, she reported, "Chief Inspector Nail had your suitcases put in #20, next door."

"Good," Margaret said. "You can yell and pound on the wall if you need us."

Malcolm went down for a key and escorted Sybil to her new quarters. Margaret could hear his voice in the hall, and then his footsteps receded toward the upper floor.

The excitement over, the two ladies hardly knew where to begin, there was so much to consider. "We didn't get any tea," Judy said. "Would you like some?"

"Oh forget tea! Did the gang tear up Sybil's room like that? How can we find out? And what about the Quists and their jewelry?"

"Will Goldy be arrested, now that Richard has decided to talk?" Judy plopped into the chair, holding her head.

"Maybe I'd like tea, after all." Margaret started the kettle and tried to organize her whirling thoughts. The water still tasted metallic, but the hot tea did help. "I just can't think. My brain's had all it can handle. What do you say we let it rest and try again tomorrow; let our subconscious minds work on it while we sleep."

"Yes, you're right. Take two aspirins and call me in the morning."

Judy got ready for bed and picked up *The Happy Prisoner.* "Do you mind if I read your book?"

Margaret did take an aspirin—only one—then filled the tub and luxuriated in steamy bubble bath, finishing with a henna shampoo and rinse under the spout. When she emerged from the bathroom, warm and relaxed, Judy's eyes were closed and the book lay face down on her bosom, still clasped in both hands. Margaret carefully dislodged it and laid it aside, then turned off the light and sat on her bed in the dark, rubbing her hair with a towel.

Judy only dozed. Suddenly, she sat straight up in bed and announced, "It was Goldy! I saw her go up the stairs!"

"What are you talking about?"

"While we were at dinner—I saw her plain as anything, going upstairs, carrying a shopping bag. I only saw her back, but it was Goldy, all right. She had an old black coat on and her hair covered with a scarf. She looked like a cleaning woman! Margaret, it was Goldy who searched Sybil's room!"

On Tuesday morning, with the inquest scheduled for 10:00 A.M., Margaret took time after breakfast for her own affairs.

"Good morning, Mrs. Canady." She stopped at the front desk. "Could I borrow your telephone book for a few minutes?"

Poldark, the black cat, walked across the counter and poked his nose into her face in a familiar way. She petted his arched back, and he purred loudly.

"Yes, Mrs. Millet. Here you are."

The fat telephone book covered the entire Cornish Peninsula. If Penfolds were still to be found in England, they should be listed here. Margaret carried the book to a bench beside the newspaper racks.

"Mrs. Millet—oh, I am glad to see you!" Molly Arvin had just pulled a paper from the coin-operated rack.

The stench of stale tobacco assaulted Margaret's nostrils. Does she have any idea how her breath smells? As though she could read the thought, Molly popped a breath mint into her mouth—and lit a cigarette.

"Everything is so awful. Can I talk to you? Do you mind?"

Lean, stringy, and deeply tanned, Molly had the heavy smoker's blotchy skin and stained fingers. Dark smudges underscored her eyes, and her voice rasped, deep and husky, like a man with a bad cold. Vocal cords destroyed—bet she has no sense of taste or smell left at all, Margaret thought. "Good morning." She patted the bench beside her. "Sit down. Of course you can talk to me."

"I wanted to go to Mass this morning, but Jake wouldn't let me," Molly complained. "Of course he never converted—my parents still say we're living in sin, after all these years."

Margaret mumbled sympathetically, but couldn't comment on the religious disagreements of a lifetime.

Molly went on. "He's been so strange ever since that man Budge was killed. When they made us stay for the inquest—well, I try to do my duty and help my husband, but I don't think we should tell lies, do you?"

"No, I don't. The police need the truth if they are to solve the case. What does he want you to lie about?"

Molly looked frightened and quickly reversed herself. "Oh no, not really lie! I just mean... Jake says that if it has nothing to do with the murder, why complicate things? He says all I have to do is say we were together, and then he won't have to go into a lot of things that don't matter. Of course, I see that, but still..."

Jake Arvin had no alibi! Margaret did her best to stay calm and casual, making her next remark a statement, not a question. "You mean the night of Budge's death."

"Well, he just took a walk around town. He... Jake likes to walk at night. He says you get the real feel of a place when you walk it at night, alone. He finds places he wants to use and goes back later with his camera. He did that in Bath, too. Jake's really nuts about making movies. It's his thing. I always say he'd push me off a cliff if it would make a good picture." Molly laughed at her family joke, then sobered. "I guess that's not so funny, right now."

Margaret never hesitated to give good advice. "Tell the truth at the inquest, Molly. It will save trouble in the long run. Someone may have seen Jake on his rambles, and think how that would look if the police found out later. Try to get Jake to tell the truth, too."

"Thanks, dear. I feel better just talking to you. It really won't matter, though, will it? I mean, it's not as though..." The fear came back to her face. "Gee, Jake will wonder why it's taking me so long to get him a paper."

She legged it for the stairs, leaving Margaret to consider the news that Jake Arvin, he of the fanatical green eyes, was unaccounted for at the times of both murders. Molly had been wearing a long sleeved sweater, but it didn't quite cover the purple bruise marks on her wrists. Margaret remembered that other green-eyed man she had known, in her long-ago youth. That one had followed her off the bus one night and made an earnest effort to seduce her on her own front porch.

Poldark jumped up beside her on the bench. She rubbed his ears absently and turned to the Cornwall telephone book. Three Penfolds were listed; James, Jesse, and Maud—all names that occurred in her family tree! She carefully copied the names, addresses, and telephone numbers on an old envelope from her purse. She'd make her calls after the inquest.

The Coroner presided in the County Courtroom. A stern man with a wealth of experience in his age lined face, he allowed no hi-jinks from spectators or the press. Once the seats were filled, a policeman firmly stopped the curious who sought entry and closed the door.

Margaret, seated at the side with the other witnesses, was relieved to see no coffin in the room. She hadn't been quite sure that a British inquest wouldn't literally "sit upon the body."

A nine-member panel filled the jury box after being rapidly sworn in. Quite a lot of organizing went into this affair, Margaret thought. It seemed very efficient.

After the official preliminaries, Chief Inspector Nail took the witness chair, was duly sworn, and began his testimony.

"At approximately 9:45 A.M. on Thursday, 27th September, a call came into the Penzance Police Station from Dr. Harris. I took the call personally, and Dr. Harris told me he had examined the deceased, Mr. Anthony Budge, and suspected suicide by poison. I called you, Sir (to the Coroner), and together with Sergeant Morgan, we proceeded to the scene.

"Evidence at the scene made me suspect foul play, rather than suicide. The deceased had written a cheerful postcard to his mother, which I now submit into evidence." The card was produced and passed to the Coroner. "The deceased had also washed three pairs of boxer shorts and hung them on the shower rod to dry. This did not seem the sort of thing a man would do if he contemplated suicide. Inquiries were made and, as other witnesses will testify, the deceased seemed to be in good spirits at dinner the night before, with no indication of a suicidal state of mind."

"Was there any sign of a struggle? Had he been robbed?" the Coroner asked.

Nail referred to his notebook. "There is reason to believe that the deceased had received something valuable in the post. Witnesses will testify that he picked up a small package. No sign of this package or its unknown contents was found at the scene, but there was no indication of a struggle or a search. The bed was the only thing disturbed, probably by the deceased."

After Nail finished, Dr. Harris testified at length, saying nothing that Margaret didn't know. The Coroner put the autopsy report into evidence, called the poison jatrophin and admitted that it was only tested for because of information from persons on the tour. Margaret caught Judy's eye and they shared a moment of gratification.

Goldy Greening was the next witness. She squirmed her flesh into the witness chair and held her head high. The orange hair looked fresh from the beauty parlor, its color more flagrant than ever, right down to the scalp. Her face was a made up mask, lit only by the busy little eyes that darted over the witnesses and reporters.

"Just on holiday, Sir," she said in answer to the Coroner's questions. "No, never laid eyes on this Anthony Budge before the trip."

The Coroner said, "Duly noted. Step down."

Margaret gasped and bent toward Judy. "Is he going to let her get away with that?" Judy shook her head without speaking, as Goldy tossed the tail of her fox stole over one shoulder and made a dramatic exit from the box.

"Next witness!" The Coroner glared at them.

Judy's name was called and she stepped forward to be sworn. Strangely enough, no questions were asked about finding Budge's satchel in her suitcase. The Coroner took her through the discovery of the body, the parcel Budge had received in the mail, and her eye-witness account of the scene in the New Forest, when Budge offered the Barbados purge nuts to Freddie Factor.

"Unfortunately," the Coroner said, "Mr. Factor is not available for questioning. Next witness."

"Mrs. Margaret Millet."

Inspector Lamb stood up and made hand gestures like an athlete calling "time out." The Coroner looked at the clock behind his desk and said, "I'll question this witness after lunch. Inquest adjourned until 2:00 P.M. Witnesses are warned not to discuss this matter outside the Court Room."

The reporters charged out and the witnesses were led through a side door. Margaret saw Chief Inspector Nail and Inspector Lamb approach the Coroner and engage him in earnest conversation. She would have given a good deal to hear what they said.

Outside the building, Malcolm waited, square and stalwart in the bright sun and tangy air of an autumn day by the sea. He had been inside too, seated in the front row of spectators, never taking his eyes off Sybil except to scout the room's occupants for someone who might mean her harm. How can she not love this man? Margaret thought. I love him, myself. Someone to count on. Someone to trust. If I had Sybil's youth and beauty—or even just her youth! But at that age, I didn't appreciate the Malcolms either, if I knew any. Like most girls, I only appreciated them after I'd been married to someone else for years.

"Lunch?" Malcolm moved toward them.

"Walk." Sybil turned toward the Esplanade and Malcolm walked beside her. They seemed to communicate without words. Margaret and Judy watched them go.

"Well. That was interesting," Judy remarked.

"They don't need us. Let's get something to eat. All that talk has made me hungry. Thirsty, too."

They entered a nearby pub and ordered sandwiches and half-pints of lager in the best British fashion. After lunch, they strolled about, enjoying the slanted warmth of the sun.

They returned to the courtroom at 2:00 P.M., expecting the inquest to resume. The Coroner announced, "At the request of the Penzance Police, this inquest is adjourned, pending the results of criminal proceedings. The jury is excused. The witnesses will please remain, to help the police in their investigations."

He banged his gavel and the attending officers began to clear the room, amid loud protests from the press.

When the spectators were gone, Chief Inspector Nail approached Goldy Greening. "Mrs. Greening, you are under arrest for perjury before this inquest. You have the right to remain silent..." He read her rights and, backed by two uniformed men, moved her through the side entrance.

Goldy went, but not quietly. "I want to call my lawyer. You can't do this, you clown! Grunt, do something," she yelled as she disappeared from view.

Chapter 23
Mrs. Millet: The Lady's Maid

Back in their room after the inquest, Margaret said, "I'm so frustrated. I hoped we might learn something and then they stopped it just when things were getting interesting."

"You didn't get to testify," Judy commented. "Well, they didn't let me say much, either."

"How about a walk? Plenty of time before dinner."

"Why don't we stop rushing around and take a nap this afternoon." Judy slipped off her shoes and stretched out on her bed with a deep sigh.

"Well..." Margaret eyed her friend anxiously. Judy? Resting in the middle of the afternoon? "Okay. Guess I could use a lie down, at that." She plopped on the bed, covered with a down comforter about five feet long by four wide and almost two inches thick. "Gee, this is comfortable. Didn't feel this good last night—the springs left a map on my body. Hey, I wonder..."

She stripped off the bed clothes, spread the comforter on the offending mattress and covered it with the bottom sheet. Nestling into the result, she said, "Wonderful. You ought to try this." The soft quilt filled the hollows in the elderly mattress and padded its springs admirably. Margaret got up and added the top sheet and blanket.

"Such energy." Judy lay still, eyes closed.

Margaret lay down again. She was not sleepy. The people at the inquest paraded through her head, defying her to interpret their facial expressions and their words. Goldy Greening, taking the witness chair with such disdain, denying any knowledge of Budge, wiping the pouches under her eyes and waving her handkerchief at the reporters. Victor Quist on the side bench, one arm over Vicky's shoulder, whispering in Vicky's ear, the two of them united in their detachment. Jake Arvin, exposed without his video camera, following the proceedings intently, while Molly squirmed nervously at his side.

Oh, bother. She hadn't gone to the bathroom. Margaret bobbed out of bed again, hoping the weird and sporadic English toilet would flush for her. It didn't. She lifted the tank top and looked inside. "Wow, if Frank Morell could see this!" (Frank was her plumber back home.) "A U-tube—it must act as a siphon." She pressed the handle firmly, with no result. She pumped it again. And again. The siphon caught, water gushed, and she clanked the cover back into place. It bore a notice, "Flush if you must." Taking up Judy's eyebrow pencil she crossed out "must" and wrote "can."

"What are you doing in there," Judy called from the bedroom. "Why don't you go for a walk!"

Margaret sauntered into Chapel Street, headed downhill. Coming to an old stone church, she noticed a footpath through the adjoining graveyard made a short-cut to Queen Street and the Esplanade. As she passed the church, friendly natives greeted her from the side entrance.

"Hullo—fine day," observed a hearty, red faced man about her own age.

She gave him a warm smile. "A fine day for a walk. Are you going into the church? Could I see inside?"

"A tourist lady, then." The other man, taller and younger than the first. "From the States? What part?"

Margaret found this question hard to answer. She considered California her home, but had come to England from the Oregon Coast. She mentally flipped a coin and said, "Brinyside, Oregon."

"Oregon—that's in the Midwest, I think? Fine country!"

"We haven't the key—waiting for the Sexton. We're going to ring the bells."

"Oh. Well, perhaps another time." Margaret waved her hand and walked on, stopping here and there to read the tombstones along the path. Dates in the 1700s and even earlier; this graveyard could have existed before my ancestors left Cornwall. I must come back and look for Penfolds, she thought.

She wanted to call the Penfold telephone numbers, too, but for now, it was good to turn off her mind and exercise her legs. The westerly breeze had freshened and broken clouds scudded over Mount's Bay. Turning onto Queen Street, she quickened her pace.

Two people jogged along the Esplanade. Two familiar people in running shoes and turquoise nylon exercise suits—the Quists.

She reached the Esplanade as the Quists jogged by the Monarch Hotel, three blocks away. Were they just jogging, or were they going somewhere? Margaret lengthened her stride to keep them in sight. They were headed toward the fishing villages of Newlyn and Mousehole, on the west side of Mount's Bay. There were boats in those harbors, boats that could cross the Channel. And the Quists dealt in antique jewelry.

She passed a bowling green where a game was in progress. The west end of Penzance was definitely the high rent district; the houses got larger and farther apart as she went. The Esplanade ended in a flight of steps, descending to a path along the shore. The Quists had taken the path so Margaret did too, watching the bouncing, turquoise figures as they lengthened their lead.

The beach was all shingle here; round, black pebbles instead of sand. Wild asters edged the path, just like the ones that bloomed every fall in Brinyside, with yellow centers and delicate lavender petals. Did some Englishman carry aster seeds all the way to Oregon? Why else would they bloom, just the same, on the other side of the world? Margaret loved these flowers and felt a closeness, a home feeling, at finding them here. So much about Penzance was comfortable and homelike. She bent down to examine the asters more closely.

When she looked back to the path, the Quists had vanished from sight.

I'll catch up to them if they stop at the fishing harbor in Newlyn, she thought. I've got my second wind now and can walk till the cows come home.

When she reached Newlyn, the clouds had formed a gray roof overhead. The sun slanted under it from the West, making a golden path on the dark water. After her long hike, Margaret needed refreshment. She entered a pub overlooking the docked fishing boats, and ordered a half of lager. She didn't see the Quists; maybe they had jogged on to Mousehole.

The pub was nearly empty. Two weather-beaten men sat in the back corner, sipping their pints and minding their own business in the way she thought of as typically English. She perched on a bar stool and smiled as the bartender served her. He smiled back.

"A fine day for a walk," she said, just as she had to the bell ringers. He identified her origins just as quickly.

"Wot's a lady from America doing in Newlyn, then?" He looked at her curiously and stroked his fine moustache.

"Is my accent really that bad?"

"Nah ow, I wouldn't say that. But you haven't been in before—I knows me customers, you see—and you don't sound like us Cornish folk, now do you? Don't get me wrong." He polished his hands on his short, grubby apron. "I can understand you—yes, you're quite understandable. Not like some Americans. Actually, you've got hardly any accent at all..."

"Thank you, I think. Americans speak differently in different parts of the country, you know. Southerners drawl and Easterners speak terribly fast. In Brooklyn they still say 'deze and doze.' I'm from the West Coast, where we use standard television English, mostly." She sipped the beer. A little sweet for her taste, but drinkable.

"Did you know," the bartender said portentously, as though he was about to let her in on some tremendous secret, "Did you know that years ago, in the last century, all the families in Newlyn emigrated to America? Every one, all together, they went to the new country. Fact. And three years later, they all came back again. What do you think of that?" He stood back from the bar expansively, a tall, youngish man with a big head of bushy brown hair.

Margaret thought she was having her leg pulled. She grinned, shook her head, and took her beer to a seat by the window. And was immediately glad she had. At the dock, on the third fishing boat down, two figures emerged from the deck cabin and debarked, climbing over the boat rail in their turquoise jogging suits. The Quists! Getting off a fishing boat! She pulled back from the window as Vicky glanced her way and started to breathe again when they turned in the other direction and strolled off.

She could see the name across the boat's stern: LADY'S MAID, Mount's Bay. A curious name for a fishing boat. When the Quists were out of sight, Margaret left her beer behind and scuttled to the red phone booth outside the pub. She fumbled in her pockets for coins. The phone took a fifty-pence piece, a large, awkward coin that had to be firmly inserted at the right moment to make the connection, and the number for the Penzance Police Department was printed before her eyes on a card listing "Emergency Numbers."

"May I speak to Inspector Lamb, please. It's urgent! This is Margaret Millet."

She was asked to hold, and a moment later a gruff voice said, "Chief Inspector Nail here. Mrs. Millet, what can I do for you?"

Her heart sank. Chief Nail—what rotten luck! "Chief Inspector, how lucky to catch you in. I've just seen two of the murder suspects get off a fishing boat in Newlyn Harbor. The boat is the LADY'S MAID of Mount's Bay. They may have transferred the jewels."

"What suspects?"

"Mr. and Mrs. Quist."

"I see. And what are you doing in Newlyn Harbor, Mrs. Millet? If you don't mind my asking." Nail's voice dripped with sarcasm.

"Taking a walk. What does it matter? Don't you see, the boat may leave any minute and take the jewels across the Channel! You must stop it—hurry! The Quists are headed back to Penzance along the shore path, I think. They're on foot, wearing turquoise jogging suits. You can't miss them."

"Now, Mrs. Millet. I'll check into it, and if crime is being committed, you can trust your police to take care of it. Perhaps you could just stop by the station and give us a full report. Will you do that, Mrs. Millet?"

Oh, the infuriating, insufferable, head-patting man! Margaret raged inwardly and broke the connection, not trusting herself to say another word. Where is Christopher Lamb? Will anybody come to stop the LADY'S MAID? She went back inside the pub to drink her beer and watch the boat.

The LADY'S MAID showed no signs of life for the duration of that beer and half the next. The bartender brought the second glass without asking, and showed signs of lingering to talk, but Margaret snubbed him and continued to watch. A few minutes later, a sturdy figure in peacoat and watch cap climbed off the fishing boat and headed for the pub. Pushing open the scarred oaken door, he called, "Pint of bitter, John. How do you fancy me in the garment trade?"

"The garment trade!" the bartender roared. "Myron, lad, you are the glass of fashion! Let me look at you, now!"

"Don't laugh, John—I've just been drawed for me duds. 'Sa fact. Look here..." He pulled a folded sheet of paper from his pocket and flattened it on the bar. "Americans. What will they do next? The lady said she was going to London and get a suit of clothes made 'in the seafaring moteef', whatever that might be. She did a bunch of drawings and gave me this one. Is that the style, or is it not? I ask you!" Myron the fisherman sucked in his beer with gusto.

"The place is thick with 'em," the bartender said. "I got one right over there, drinkin' me ale. Wunner if she'd like to draw me?" He laughed uproariously.

Margaret had heard enough. With head held high, she dropped a one-pound coin on the table and walked out of the pub.

The clouds had won their battle with the sun and the breeze seemed colder and stronger. She zipped up her windbreaker, pulled her knit cap over her ears, and hurried toward Penzance with the wind at her back. Was that fisherman as simple as he seemed, or was it all an act? Would the stolen jewels soon be on their way to the Continent in that boat? Well, she had reported it and Chief Inspector Nail was right; from there on it was Police Business. No way would she go to the station and put it in writing, after his rebuff.

Nearing Penzance, she heard cascades of sound from the church bells. The ringers were pulling bell ropes with all their might, giving a concert for the town.

Margaret stopped at the front desk. "Any messages, Mrs. Canady?"

"Mrs. Hark said she'd be back soon. She went out with Miss Darington, a little while ago."

Malcolm came in, looking wind-blown and unhappy. He caught Mrs. Canady's words. "Miss Darington's gone out? Did she say where?"

"No, Mr. Trewbridge, she didn't."

"But Judy was with her," Margaret said. "Don't worry, they're all right. It must be time for tea, Malcolm. Come and have a cup with me. I've just had a strange experience and I'd like to tell you about it."

Tea was served buffet style from 4:00 to 6:00 P.M. Malcolm and Margaret filled their cups from a silver urn, took scones on china plates, and sat by the dining room windows to admire the multi-colored sunset.

Margaret related the tale of the Quists, the LADY'S MAID, and her panic call to the Penzance Police. "I don't know what to think," she added. "It's awfully clever, if they're the murderers. That fisherman didn't look capable of acting—he just looked full of fun and pleased with himself. Chief Inspector Nail must think I'm an awful fool." That was the painful part. But what else could she do, under the circumstances?

"I understand," Malcolm said, patting her hand. "You did all you could, Mrs. Millet, and we'll keep an eye on those two. Now, let's enjoy our tea. How do you like the old Bond Hotel? The place has quite a history, you know."

Margaret was glad to change the subject. "Yes it does, Malcolm and please call me Margaret, won't you? I admire the antiques. There's a linen chest on the landing that might have come out of the ark."

"I noticed it. The chambermaids pull everything out of it and put the fresh sheets on the bottom, so they'll be used in rotation. The one with the teeth was at it this morning, when I came down."

"Really? Then it wouldn't be a good hiding place, I guess. I keep looking for a place where Budge might have hidden the Darington jewels."

"Not unless it has a false bottom. You know, Budge might have stayed here. Some of the tours do—the less fancy ones. Gateway World always stops at the Monarch, but we don't know whose tour Budge used that other time, do we?"

"Oh, Malcolm! Do you think the police have checked? Let's ask Mrs. Canady—she could look back in her register, and find out if Budge stayed here!" A thrill ran through Margaret's body. Maybe she was wrong about the Quists, but here was a bit of detecting that might make up for it. Maybe Budge stayed here, and hid the Darington jewels on the premises. If only she could find them!

Chapter 24
Mrs. Hark: The Caravan

The telephone jingled, and Judy reached for it from the bed. "Hello?"

"Mrs. Hark? Sybil. Are you busy?"

"No, just resting. How can I help you?" I sound like customer service at the telephone company, she thought.

"I don't want to disturb you—but I can't find Malcolm, and I don't want to go alone. It's Richard, of course."

"It's all right, dear. What have you heard from Richard?"

"I've been to see him at the jail. They're keeping him there, and he wants me to bring some things from the caravan. Could you come with me?"

Judy could. Twenty minutes later she met Sybil in the lobby and they drove off in Richard's old jalopy, taking the main highway to the eastern outskirts of Penzance and then a narrow road between tall hedge-rows.

On the main road Sybil had urged the old flivver to keep up with traffic. Now she slowed down and asked, "Where is Mrs. Millet this afternoon?"

"She wanted to walk, so I said 'go ahead, I want a nap.' I didn't sleep much, though. Wasn't it queer, the way they cut off the inquest, and arrested Goldy?"

"I told Richard and he said, 'They do believe me, then.' If they believe him, why charge Goldy with perjury instead of robbery and murder?"

"I don't know. Maybe just to hold her until they get more evidence. Besides, it's true. Her testimony at the inquest was one big, fat lie. It took my breath away when she said she'd never met Budge before the trip."

"Here we are." Sybil drove under a wrought-iron archway sign reading TREVAR CAMP. The old car jounced in deep ruts, scraped on the hump between them, and spit gravel noisily off its nether parts. Judy clutched the armrest with both hands until Sybil braked in front of a tiny trailer.

"The fox's lair, the black sheep's fold, Brother Richard's hideaway."

Only ten or twelve feet long by six feet wide, the trailer's aluminum had oxidized to a dull grey. Its shape was dated; teardrop sides, roof sloped to a wedge-shaped tail. Streamlining was big when this trailer was built. Faded curtains blocked the windows and the door didn't quite fit any more—or it wasn't solidly latched.

Parked at the end of a row, the trailer stood on gravel, well back in a space made private by lattice fencing and tall shrubs. A bushy pine tree hid the nearest neighbor. It might have been alone in the woods, miles from any other human habitation. Judy felt reluctant to leave the car, but Sybil came around and opened her door, so she got out into the cool, pine-scented air.

Sybil rummaged in her purse for Richard's key. Judy reached past her to the door handle, a sort of lever with a lock in the center. The handle turned and the door fell toward them, hanging by one hinge, and nearly conked Sybil on the head. "Here—look out!" Judy cried. Sybil gasped and stumbled back.

It was dark inside the trailer, but Judy got an impression of bedding or clothing piled high in the doorway. Something metallic fell out, clattering as it hit gravel.

"Oh, my God..." Sybil reached inside and turned on a light, revealing wreckage. It was impossible to enter. The trailer had been destroyed as thoroughly as Sybil's hotel room and the perpetrator must have worked from back to front, piling things behind him (or her) on the way.

"Oh, Sybil, what a mess!" They stood in the light from the trailer door and by contrast, the shrubbery and trees suddenly turned to dark walls on either side. Judy listened intently as a breeze sighed through the pines and a sleepy owl, far away, asked Who-o-o?

"Who is right. Let's get out of here. They may still be around, looking for you." Judy pushed the trailer door to and pulled Sybil's arm. "Come on."

Sybil seemed rooted to the spot. She listened with younger ears than Judy Hark's. "Wait. Someone's out there."

Was that a footstep hushed by the carpet of pine needles? A twig snapped. A dark form pushed through the bushes.

"Run! Hide in the woods!" Judy yelled, pulling Sybil away from the glowing trailer windows. Sybil stumbled and sprawled in the gravel. The dark form rushed toward them behind a blinding flashlight beam.

"Stop! It's me!" The voice was familiar—and welcome, to say the least. Inspector Lamb.

"Well, why didn't you say so? Scared us half to death—what's the big idea?" Judy was too relieved to mince words.

Lamb turned his light aside and helped Sybil up. "Sorry. Sybil, are you hurt? What are you doing out here? Didn't I tell you to stay in a safe place?"

"Richard wanted some of his things." Sybil picked a chip of gravel off her knee and rubbed the wound under her torn stocking.

"What are you doing out here?" Judy demanded. "And why didn't you come sooner and catch whoever demolished this trailer?" If this sounded like she wanted it both ways, she couldn't help it. She was too upset to be fair.

"I hoped he'd come back. We didn't know about the caravan until Richard told us. By the time we got here—well, you've seen."

"And who did know about it, I might ask? Who knew this

trailer was here, and who might think Richard or Sybil had the jewels? Goldy Greening comes to mind, but she's in jail. So who, Inspector?"

"This is no time or place to talk about it, Mrs. Hark. Let's get Sybil away, first of all. Can you drive this heap? I'll follow you back to Penzance."

Sybil regained her poise. "I can drive. I'm perfectly all right. What about Richard's things?"

"Blow Richard's things! Don't come out here again—that's an order! My car's by the entrance. Wait there, so I can follow you in."

Lamb opened the trailer door and shut off the light. Sybil did as she was told, and Lamb's headlights bounced into her face from the rear view mirror, all the way back to Penzance.

"What you said, Mrs. Hark—about who knows the caravan is here—who do you think...?"

"We don't know when it was trashed. Did Richard tell Goldy where he was staying?"

"That's it, you know. He didn't. He thought the caravan was safe because nobody knew, except me. And Malcolm, when he brought me out here."

Judy said, "One of the gang could have followed Richard and found this place. It's something they'd do, I should think. They'd want to keep tabs on him."

Malcolm, she thought. Margaret will die if it turns out to be Malcolm. I wouldn't dare to suggest it. It has possibilities though. Who knew about the Darington jewels? Malcolm. Who knew where everybody stayed when the tour stopped in Penzance? Malcolm. Ah, but the night Budge was murdered, Malcolm was squiring Margaret all over the town. He couldn't have done it—unless Lamb is wrong, and he didn't stay to watch Budge die. And the night Freddie Factor met his end? Where was Malcolm then? And motive? With enough money, a man might hope to win the girl he loved, even if he wasn't in her class.

He didn't trash Sybil's hotel room; that was Goldy, I'd bet any amount on that. Would he trash the trailer, copycat fashion, to keep suspicion concentrated on the gang? He could have the Cromarth collection—and the Darington jewels, too, if he got Budge to talk. It's so complicated—like the fleas. '...all the fleas have other fleas, upon their backs to bite 'em.' "Humh? I'm, sorry, what did you say? I was wool-gathering."

"Where should I leave Richard's car?" Sybil slowed and pulled over to the curb. They were still several blocks from the Bond Hotel.

"Leave it at the police station. The Inspector can give us a ride to the hotel."

Lamb pulled up behind them and came to Sybil's window. He vetoed Judy's suggestion. "Better not advertise Richard's stay with us. Why not the hotel?"

"For the same reason. I don't want anybody looking for him there."

"Yes, I see."

Judy said, "How about the train station? If somebody sees it there, maybe they'll think Richard went away."

This seemed a good idea, and Lamb followed them to the depot. After she parked the flivver, Sybil maneuvered Judy into the front seat of the police car, then sandwiched her in.

Judy said, "About Goldy Greening, Inspector—I've been wanting to tell you—I'm sure she was the one who searched Sybil's room. I saw her from the back, going upstairs during dinner. She was dressed like a cleaning woman, but the way she moved and her size—I'm sure it was Goldy. She was carrying a big shopping bag."

Lamb showed immediate interest. "Yes, we think so, too. Her room is on the ground floor, so if you saw her going upstairs, that tends to confirm it."

"And in Disguise! I mean, compared to the way she usually dresses. A head scarf and that baggy old coat... I wonder where she got it?"

"Maybe I can find out. Thank you, Mrs. Hark. I'll inquire."

Tit for tat, Judy thought. I've given information, why not ask for some? "We wondered about the way you arrested her, Inspector. The charge of perjury?"

"That we can prove, with young Darington's help," Lamb said. "I can't hold her in jail much longer. We're scrambling for evidence to tie her to the murders before her lawyer gets her out on bail."

He added, "Goldy or Davis may have searched the caravan, Sybil. If they knew about it. Your brother says they didn't."

"I know," Sybil said. "Mrs. Hark thinks they followed Richard out there, checking up on him."

"Possible. What about your friend, the bus driver? Richard says he saw the caravan." He emphasized "friend" in a suggestive way.

"Malcolm? Malcolm has nothing to do with this mess!" Sybil reacted like a wolf-mother defending her pups.

Lamb snapped back. "Why did he come here? He wasn't summoned."

"He came on his own, purely to help. And you can interpret that any way you wish!"

They stopped in front of the hotel and Sybil flounced out of the police car and ran inside. Judy sat where she was. "Let her go, Inspector. I'll make sure she's safely in her room tonight. Poor Richard, he won't get his toothbrush."

And poor Christopher Lamb. Jealousy is terribly painful.

Chapter 25
Mrs. Hark: Anthony Budge Slept Here

Sybil had encountered Malcolm and Margaret at the foot of the stairs. Judy joined them, as Malcolm was saying, "...and Margaret thinks Budge might have stayed in this hotel after your robbery."

So it's Margaret now, Judy thought as she grasped the possibilities of Budge at the Bond. "Really! Then he could have hidden the Darington jewels here."

"Exactly," Margaret said. "We're going to ask Mrs. Canady to look in her old guest register."

At the desk, no one was visible except Poldark, asleep on the counter beside the bell. Margaret rang. Poldark stretched and turned up his tummy to be scratched. Mrs. Canady must have been having her tea; she bobbed up behind the desk still chewing and swallowing.

Margaret got right to the point. "It's about the man who was murdered. We think he might have stayed here several years ago, when he was in Penzance with a tour. When was it, Sybil?"

"The robbery was three years ago, in October."

Margaret said, "His name was Budge, but we don't know the tour company."

Mrs. Canady's lifted eyebrows said, 'So What?' and Judy intervened to spread some of the very best butter. "We're sorry to bother you, but it's truly important. Have the police asked you about this?" It is important, she thought. Margaret's right, it could be the key to the whole thing. "Could you look in the register? It would be such a help!"

"Oh... Well then, perhaps... Really, I don't know. The guest registers are supposed to be confidential."

"Of course. We understand, and we wouldn't dream of asking—but this is a case of murder. If the police have missed this, we must tell them about it. Every minute counts. Could you look now?" Judy had a way of making the person she addressed feel vitally important.

"Three years ago, in October. I'd have to get the old register out of the store room."

Margaret said, "Fine. We appreciate it. We'll be in our room, waiting to hear from you."

Judy added, "I'll see that Scotland Yard knows how helpful you've been."

Once upstairs, Sybil and Malcolm went to their own rooms, so the ladies had a chance to share the experiences of the day.

Judy went first. "It was just like Sybil's room. Richard's trailer—or caravan as the English say—was a pile of trash. They pulled every pot and dish out of the cupboards and cut open his mattress and went through his clothes—it was just awful. And when Inspector Lamb jumped out of the bushes, I thought the end had come, I really did."

Margaret was properly shocked, and roused the same emotions in Judy when she described the Quists' jog to Newlyn Harbor. "I may have made an awful fool of myself," she said. "But on the other hand, what are the police doing? They've got Goldy, but can they keep her? And they'll have to let the others leave pretty soon, won't they? They'll search everything we take with us, so the murderer must be anxious to get rid of the Cromarth collection. And why else would the Quists visit a fishing boat? Can you believe it was about clothes?"

"Clothes are important to some people, Margaret." Judy refrained from adding "even though not to you, dear friend."

"The Quists? It's hard to believe they're interested in anything but clothes. If they are, they're in it together, both of them. I just don't know. Anyway, you reported it. And checking on where Budge stayed after the Darington robbery is brilliant."

"Yes," Margaret agreed. "You know, I have a strong feeling he did stay here at the Bond. All the same, he wouldn't hide the jewels in his room; he'd hide them where he could get to them any time. Hidden in plain sight, like *The Purloined Letter*."

They talked quite a while and then dressed for dinner. Just as Judy pulled on a full, tiered skirt, in shades of lavender and purple, the phone rang. Margaret picked it up, listened briefly, and said, "I'll see that the police get the information. Whirlwind Tours. Thanks so much, Mrs. Canady."

"What did she say?"

"He was here, all right. And get this—he stayed in room 23—Sybil's room, the one they trashed!"

"By himself?"

"Of course."

"Oh, Margaret, let's call the police, right away."

"And get Chief Nail again. No thanks, I tried that earlier today. The next time I talk to him, I want proof in hand."

"What proof?" The gleam in her friend's eye made Judy suspicious.

"You'll see. Just hold off until tomorrow, okay?"

Judy let it go, but made no promises.

By unspoken agreement, they avoided the subject of crime during dinner. Inspector Lamb did not appear. The only familiar people in the dining room were Jake and Molly Arvin, at a distant table and they were at the end of their meal. Jake raised his wine glass and Molly twiddled her fingers and smiled, before they left the dining room.

Over a plate of brussels sprouts and a mystery food called "English Game Pie," Margaret talked about bell ringers and wild asters.

"No, thank you," Judy said. The plum duff desert looked

entirely too heavy; no wonder Margaret was so round in the middle. "Let's go down to the bar after dinner. Maybe the others are there; Sybil and Malcolm and the Quists. I promised Inspector Lamb I'd see Sybil safe in her room tonight. He was horrified that she went out to the trailer park."

Margaret spooned up the last bit of cream from her plum duff. "Mmmm, I needed that. I must have walked at least five miles today. And a small Drambuie would help my digestion. Yes, let's go down to the bar."

The Nelson Bar occupied the lowest level of the hotel, and two of its walls were the ancient stone of the original structure. A low beamed ceiling spanned both rooms, one strictly for drinking and the other furnished with small tables and offering pub-type food. This room had a stone fireplace, flanked by a pair of red-cushioned oak settles. The lighting was subdued, but not dim. Malcolm and Sybil sat near the fire, over the remains of their evening meal. Jake Arvin sat alone, nursing a pint mug, nearby.

The ladies got drinks at the bar, Margaret's Drambuie and white wine for Mrs. Hark, then made their way to where the young people sat.

"We have news," Margaret said.

"Do join us." Sybil moved over and Malcolm rose to bring another chair.

"Margaret was right. Budge stayed here, in this hotel. We're going to tell Inspector Lamb—has he been here?" Judy spoke in her usual clear, ringing tones, and Jake Arvin's head jerked as though struck by a sudden spasm.

"Haven't seen the Inspector," Sybil said, "and don't want to. I wish he'd quit telling me what to do." She looked tired and added little to the conversation that followed.

True to her promise, Judy saw Sybil to her room that night, but not inside, because Margaret drew her away, whispering, "Let her say goodnight to Malcolm."

Inside their room they heard Sybil say "Goodnight, then," and sounds of her door being locked and bolted. Malcolm stood in the hall briefly, then thumped up the stairs. Margaret's face fell in disappointment and Judy thought, well! Look who's match-making now!

Chapter 26
Mrs. Millet: Accents of Brooklyn

Her walk to Newlyn Harbor had left Margaret Millet more than willing to go to bed early. Let's see, she thought, by 2:00 A.M. that first, heavy sleep will be over and I'll be capable of alertness again. She told her mental clock to wake her then, and just in case, she set her travel alarm for 2:30.

And if Judy is having her insomnia again, maybe I can persuade her to come along. I'll cross that bridge when I come to it. Good thing she didn't see me filch the "tools."

At 2:15, Margaret raised her head. Her internal clock had worked within the time allowed. She turned off the alarm, pushed her feet into her terry scuffs, and pulled on her traveling robe, a light weight "happy coat" that took little space in a suitcase. Br-r-r, she thought, the room is cold, but Judy will wake up for sure if I try to get dressed. I hope the halls are warmer.

The only light came through the transom, but she could see well enough to find her purse and transfer a sturdy table-knife and a two-pronged serving fork, purloined from the bar, to the pocket of her robe. She grasped her flash light and eased the hall door open with only the slightest click of the latch. Judy slept on, wheezing a little, her face as relaxed as a child's in the light from the doorway.

I'll start here and work my way down. She peered under the little table beside her door. She put a hand down inside a large urn near the stairs, but felt only the dusty prickle of the dried grasses and peacock feathers it contained. Her eyes roamed the walls and ceiling of the hallway, then the carpet and baseboards. Hidden in an accessible spot. But where? On to her main objective, the linen chest on the landing, an ideal hiding place. Beautiful, noticeable, steadily in use. And permanent, never moved.

There were lights both above and below, but the landing itself was in deep shadow. Margaret poked the two-pronged fork underneath the front of the chest, gently feeling its bottom for any irregularity. She could only get the fork about a third of the way in. She'd have to pull the chest away from the wall. Ugh, too heavy. Well then, unload it first, and look inside.

Something creaked in the lobby below and Margaret froze, holding her breath and listening with all her ears; ears that still worked very well. She heard her own heartbeat, loud and fast. Old buildings always creak at night, she told herself. Contractions from changes in temperature. When her heart settled down, she lifted the carved lid, took out sheets, towels, and pillowcases and piled them on the landing.

The huge chest was lined with cedar and in spite of its great age, a whiff of woodsy perfume reached Margaret's nose as she worked her way down to the bottom. She bent from the hips, nearly double, to lift out the last layer of neatly folded wool blankets. The blankets smelled more strongly of cedar. Maybe they weren't taken out every day like the sheets and towels.

She laid them aside and bent into the chest again, shining her flash on the bottom boards and probing the interstices between them with the table-knife's thin blade. The joinery was still tight, after all these years. A beautiful piece of craftsmanship, given the way cedar absorbs and gives off moisture. Ah, was that a crack? The knife blade found room to slip through, stopping solidly two inches later. There was a space between the lining and the bottom! And tiny scratches, as though this board had been worked at before. Three inches wide, six inches long.

Would it come up? Not from the side with the knife blade. She tried the two-prong fork. With this jammed at one end of the board and the knife at the other, she worked it gently up until her fingers could grasp it and pull it free.

Bubble wrap! Is it the jewels, or just insulation? Nonsense, bubble wrap was unknown when this chest was built; it has to be the jewels! She pulled and pried and twisted until a plastic packet suddenly came free. She loosened the tape and wrappings at one end, exposing the luster of pearls, and raised up in triumph, too excited to notice the shadow that had fallen over her from behind.

Margaret's skull exploded in a flash of pain and she fell, head down, into the open chest.

The murderer left her dangling, pocketed the cosh, and picked up the packet of jewels. She'd be safe for hours, tapped on just the right spot. And she never saw a thing.

As he died, Budge had said, "bon... in chess." The Bond Hotel, in a chest. So here we are.

The jewels were irresistible. The killer opened the packet and pulled gently on a strand of the Hortensia pearls until the entire rope, held aloft, gleamed in milky splendor. Perfectly matched, separated by tiny jade beads, breathtakingly lovely. The diamond sunburst was next, softly blazing with its own light. Smaller pieces, each wrapped in ordinary facial tissue.

Best not to linger. The pearls went into a bathrobe pocket and the rest back into the bubble wrap. Margaret was lifted and laid face-up on the floor. She'd sleep longer in a comfortable position.

Margaret knew she was dreaming but she couldn't stop, couldn't wake up. Like coming out of anesthesia, the fogs and vapors in her brain kept pulling her back into the dream. Freddie Factor put his face close to hers (she could smell his revolting after-shave), and sang "sittin' on da coib, at toity toid and toid, eatin' doity woims," over and over, faster and faster, in his nasal,

Brooklyn voice.

"Americans speak differently in different parts of the country, you know," she said to the bartender in the Newlyn pub.

Then she was in the chemistry lab of her college days, with a bratty, student lab-assistant scrawling on the chalkboard. He drew a first grader's tree—well, maybe a second grader's tree—broad roots, tall trunk, a top like a billow of cloud. Beside it, he drew a little mound of flattened circles. Then a large plus sign and another tree, another mound. And repeat; plus sign, tree, mound. He turned with a broad grin and said, "Don't you get it?" What was that kid's name? Tommy, that was it, Tommy. Tommy danced around in her swirling brain and chanted, "Tree and a turd, plus tree and a turd, plus tree and a turd, equals ten! Ha ha, ha ho! Add 'em up, equals ten, equals ten!"

She fell again into nothingness, a blank void that left Tommy behind, getting smaller and smaller until he disappeared.

She was cold, very cold. Her bones hurt on the hard, unyielding floor. If only her eyes would open. The attempt caused an agonizing flash through her skull and another retreat, only partial this time, into the darkness. Freddie came back, but in a rational way. He turned on the woodsy path in St. Ives, muttering, "check da tree-I, check da tree-I. Check da tree-eye!" as he went.

At last, Margaret was able to move. She rolled onto one side and pushed herself up to a sitting position on the cold carpet of the landing, rubbing the goose bumps on her arms. She felt gingerly of the egg-sized lump behind her right ear. The chest was still open, the linens still in piles on the floor. I'll have to tidy up, she thought hazily, then realized she should leave things as they were and call Inspector Lamb. She knew now, who had murdered Tony Budge and Freddie Factor. Freddie had told her.

Chapter 27
Mrs. Hark: Lost and Found

At 4:00 A.M. Judy Hark's eyes opened wide and stared at the ceiling. This often happened and at home she coped with night-time wakefulness by reading until she got sleepy again. During this trip, she had suffered her bouts of insomnia without relief, not wanting to disturb Margaret. It is fun to travel with Margaret, she thought. I'll think about her and the trip—not the murders, the trip. Maybe I can get back to sleep again before my entire life begins to parade past me. She turned on her side, expecting to see Margaret's tousled head on her pillow—and saw only the empty bed. Margaret was not there!

Alarmed, Judy flung the covers aside and got up. She pulled on her traveling slippers and robe and opened the door. Stumbling footsteps on the stairs; a figure rose slowly into view, clutching the banister. Margaret. Thank God.

"Where the dickens have you been? Scared me to death—I woke up and you were gone. Oh, Margaret! Are you all right?"

Margaret tottered into the room and made it to the bed. "No. Call Inspector Lamb. I've been bashed on the head and the killer's got the jewels. I led him right to them."

"Bashed on the head! I'll call a doctor..." Judy snapped on the light and dashed to the telephone.

Margaret covered her eyes. "No, Judy. Listen. No doctor—just Inspector Lamb." She lay over sideways on the bed and groaned. "I know who the murderer is. Call Inspector Lamb."

Quickly, Judy dialed Lamb's room number. After five agonizing rings, he growled, "Lamb here."

"This is Judy Hark. Please come to our room, Inspector. Margaret's been hurt. Hurry! Please!"

"Hurt? What happened? What about Sybil?"

"Not on the phone. We're not in immediate danger, but come as fast as you can." Judy hung up and turned to her friend. "He'll be right here. Let me see that head."

Margaret put her hand to the lump and Judy carefully parted the hair to inspect it. "No broken skin. What did he hit you with? Did you see who it was? What on earth were you doing?" Good grief, Margaret could have been killed with as little compunction as was shown to Freddie Factor.

"Trying to find the jewels—finding the jewels. I had them in my hand when he hit me." Margaret grimaced and sagged against the pillow. "Wait for Lamb. I can't tell it twice."

Judy bustled into the bathroom and squeezed out one of their new wash cloths in cold water. "Sorry I don't have an ice bag, but maybe this will help. How about an aspirin? You're shivering! Get under the covers!"

When Inspector Lamb rapped on the door, Margaret was as comfortable as Judy could make her, full of aspirin and propped up on the pillows to drink a steaming cup of tea. Her color was better and her voice almost normal.

"Well, what's all this, then?" Lamb asked. He hadn't hurried. He was completely dressed and had even shaved.

"Sit down, Inspector. Margaret's been out prowling and got bashed on the head. She hasn't told me yet, either." Judy handed Lamb their second cup, a real sacrifice, as she needed the tea herself.

"I found the Darington Jewels, Inspector. In the linen chest on the landing. That's where they were, hidden under a cedar board in the bottom of it. I'd just got the packet out and one end of it open when somebody hit me from behind and knocked me out."

"Did you get a look at him?"

"No. I had no idea he was there until he hit me. I didn't hear or see a thing. But Inspector, I know who it was. I'm absolutely sure I know who it was."

Inspector Lamb sat back and waited for the revelation with a skeptical face. Margaret seemed aware of his skepticism and not in the least intimidated.

"It's because of Freddie Factor, you see—something he said that I didn't understand at the time. Remember, Judy, when we were in St. Ives, and he met us on that path below the hotel—when he told us he'd seen somebody fooling around with the suitcases, the morning after Budge's murder."

"I remember it perfectly," Judy said. "I got the impression that he knew who it was, but he wouldn't tell us."

"No, he wouldn't say, and he went off muttering something that sounded like 'tree I,' which made no sense at all. 'Got to check d' tree I' were his exact words, Inspector."

"You're quite right. It makes no sense at all." Lamb sipped his tea with exaggerated patience. Judy wondered, where is Margaret going with this?

"The thing is, you have to translate it from the Brooklyn-ese. While I was waking up from this," she felt the lump tenderly, "my brain did the translation. Have you ever heard a little ditty that goes, Sittin' on da coib, at toity toid and toid, eatin' doity woims?"

Lamb smiled and shook his head.

"Well, I have, and other similar sayings. Anyhow, what Freddie said translates to 'Got to check the three-eye.' Now who do we know on the tour who might be referred to as the three-eye?"

"Jake Arvin and his video camera!" Judy got it in one. "Oh, yes. And last night in the bar—" She saw an instant picture of Jake's involuntary twitch when she announced that Budge had stayed at the Bond Hotel. She told Lamb and added, "He's not stupid. He must have realized that the Darington jewels might be hidden here. I'll bet he was looking for them too, Margaret!"

"You should arrest him immediately, Inspector."

"Now hold on. This isn't half interesting, but it's not evidence. I can't arrest Jake Arvin because Factor said something about a three eye."

Lamb emptied his cup, but Judy was past caring about tea. Oh, the stupidity of policemen! "But you must! He knows the jewels have been seen—he'll escape! He may have already escaped!"

"Not that lad. Assuming for one minute that you're right about him, he knows we haven't a thing on him. He won't bolt."

Margaret said, "If he's caught with the jewels on him—don't you see? It's the only way. You must arrest him before he can get rid of them!"

"Mrs. Millet, let me bring you up to date. The police have not been idle. We have not left it to you ladies to catch our criminals for us, although we thank you for your wonderful efforts. Two sure things in a day and a night! I do admire your energy and dedication, but we already have our guilty parties in jug. The professionals, Mrs. Millet, the professionals. The professional burglar who stole the Cromarth collection has been caught handily in London—in the act of committing another burglary. He's singing his head off. He's fingered our friend Goldy Greening, and with his testimony and young Darington's, we're going to put her inside for a long time. Conspiracy, grand larceny, and a fistful of other charges. So far, we don't have the physical evidence to tie her and Davis to the murders, but we'll find it, no fear."

"But the jewels, Inspector—I saw them—the Darington jewels! They were in the chest!"

"Did you actually see them, Mrs. Millet? Did you have them in your hands?"

"Not in my hands, but I opened one end of the packet. Something white, like pearls, was plainly visible. And who hit me on the head?"

"We'll look into that, of course. I suggest you see a doctor as soon as possible. Meanwhile I submit, dear lady, that you saw what you wanted to see. Perhaps you got so excited that you fell down the stairs?"

Margaret gasped and Lamb rose apologetically and opened the door. "Oh, I forgot to tell you—the skipper of the LADY'S MAID is Chief Inspector Nail's brother-in-law. He never smuggled anything in his life." Lamb walked out and gently closed the door. Margaret buried her face in the pillow.

Judy was horrified by Lamb's stupidity and Margaret's despair. "Unbearable! I'm so sorry, dear. Rest, now. We'll figure something out—we're not going to let him get away with it, I promise." Whether "him" was Inspector Lamb or Jake Arvin, she wasn't sure at that moment. Maybe both of them!

Margaret lifted her head. "You do believe me, don't you Judy? It is Jake Arvin, I know it is. Molly's given him an alibi, but she didn't know where he was when Budge died, or the night Freddie was killed, either. He's kept her quiet by force—I saw the bruises. Lamb didn't give me a chance to tell him. He wouldn't listen." She wailed, "Oh, I give up!" and turned away.

"Of course I believe you. It's our possibility number four, isn't it? Someone Budge knew, someone on the tour, someone Freddie saw in the hall and identified. Try to sleep, Margaret. I'll go down for breakfast in a little while and bring you back a tray."

Judy picked up the wet wash cloth and smoothed the blankets around Margaret's body, patting her shoulder in a comforting way. Then she made herself a cup of tea and sat in the chair to think. Margaret didn't move. Good. The best thing, after all she'd been through, was rest.

At eight o'clock, Judy hung the DO NOT DISTURB card on the door and went down to breakfast. She stopped at the desk and told Mrs. Canady not to bother Margaret with telephone calls. "Just take a message, please. She's had a bad night."

"She's not the only one," Mrs. Canady said. "Someone's been rootling through the linen chest, and I've only just got it straightened up. What goings on—first that young lady's room torn apart, and now the linen chest! What next? Just see if we take any more policemen and witnesses and such! Not that you ladies are any trouble... I don't mean that..."

"Oh my, yes. It must be very difficult for you." Judy shook her head and walked quickly away before any more calumnies could be related. Breakfast. She needed food. Perhaps food would lead to ideas.

When Judy carried a tray up to Margaret, she met Molly Arvin on the stairs. Molly passed her with a quick "Good morning," and walked rapidly toward the Chapel Street door. She carried a tote-bag with a square parcel in it, wrapped in brown paper. Judy set the tray on the linen chest and reached the door in time to see Molly turn up the hill, in the direction of the shops—and the post office!

Margaret's breakfast would have to wait. Oh, where were the police when you needed them? When Molly was well up the street, she pushed through the door and followed, keeping close to the buildings. Coatless, she shivered in the brisk wind. The shops were opening, and people began to block her view. She lengthened her stride. Molly looked anxiously behind her and Judy dodged behind the other pedestrians.

The post office it was. Molly and her tote-bag went through the main door, and Judy circled to the side and looked in. Molly joined a longish line of early patrons in front of the only active window.

Judy went in and grasped Molly's arm—the arm holding the tote-bag. "Molly, I know what's in your parcel."

Startled, Molly tried to free her arm. "Video tapes," she said, "just video tapes. Jake's used so many we have to mail them home. No more room in the suitcases." She giggled.

"Is that what he told you?" Judy lowered her voice; no use

involving innocent bystanders. "Molly, there's stolen property in those video cassettes. If you mail them, you are abetting a crime. Crimes. Robbery and murder."

"Oh, no! No, no, no!"

"Yes. You know it, don't you Molly? You know Jake and you know what he's done. You mustn't mail them. Come with me to the police station—it's only a couple of blocks."

It took persuasion, but in the end, Molly came.

Judy unwrapped the parcel in Chief Inspector Nail's office, opened the cleverly reworked cassettes, spilled out their contents, and separated the packing from the treasure. It made a dazzling display on Nail's desk; the carved splendor of the Cromarth emeralds, Ophelia Darington's diamond sunburst, the Hortensia pearls, the smaller pieces, the loose diamonds and rubies, all laid out in rows. Inspector Lamb came in while this was going on and stared at the jewels, open-mouthed. As did Chief Inspector Nail.

Judy's only regret was that Margaret Millet couldn't see their faces.

Chapter 28
Mrs. Millet: Things of Beauty

Margaret Millet woke up sore all over and hungry for her promised breakfast. It was nearly ten o'clock. A hot bath eased the soreness, and she dressed comfortably in jeans and pullover, thinking who cares how I look, anyway? People are getting away with murder around here—why should I dress up? The lump on her head had gone down a little but was still very tender. She gently combed her hair to hide it and took another aspirin.

On her way downstairs she noticed the breakfast tray on the linen chest, the oatmeal porridge cold and congealed. Strange—and alarming. Where was Judy?

"Have you seen Mrs. Hark?" she asked at the desk.

"Good morning, Mrs. Millet. Yes, Mrs. Hark came by and said not to disturb you. Mr. Trewbridge asked about you, but I told him what Mrs. Hark said, and he didn't leave any message. How are you feeling?"

"Oh, I'm fine, thank you. But Judy left my breakfast on the linen chest—some time ago, I think—where can she have gone?"

"Why, I don't know, dear. Don't worry, I'm sure she's all right."

Margaret also felt that Judy could take care of herself. Something had happened, though. Judy would have a tale to tell when she showed up. The idea heartened her and she asked, "Is it too late for breakfast? I'm starved."

"They've stopped serving in the dining room, but you can always get something in the Nelson Bar."

She was devouring bacon and eggs when Judy found her. She saw that Judy was bursting with news. "Sit. Tell."

"Oh Margaret, will I!" The story tumbled out, how Molly had tried to mail the jewels away, how perfectly they were hidden in the video cassettes, how dumbfounded Inspector Lamb and Chief Inspector Nail had been when she poured them out on Nail's desk.

Margaret glowed. Trust Judy to deliver the goods! Only she could have figured it out so quickly, acted so effectively, and persuaded Molly to cooperate. What a woman!

"You're wonderful! Just wonderful! And have they picked up Jake?"

"Yes. Molly said she was to meet him at a coffee shop on the Esplanade, but when they got there he was gone. They caught him at the railroad station, just getting on the London train. I sat right there in the Chief's office and heard everything on their radio, as Inspector Lamb chased him down. And Margaret, Chief Nail was just wonderful! He was so sweet... and apologized so nicely!"

Margaret pictured the burly Chief Inspector Nail, down on his knees in sweet apology. She began to laugh and couldn't stop; the picture was too hilarious, the relief of being vindicated too great. She laughed and giggled and chortled until people in the bar turned to stare and Judy stopped laughing with her and patted her back in concern.

"Here, take a drink of water. I shouldn't have sprung it on you all at once, like that."

Margaret lowered her head and gradually regained control. The picture of Chief Nail recurred and caused small eruptions until she put it resolutely away and wiped her eyes. "Oh, that did me good. What wouldn't I give to have seen them..." Laughter threatened again, but she subdued it.

"Then Chief Nail called the man who was robbed, Sir somebody Cromarth, and he's coming to identify his jewels. He should get here late this afternoon. Sybil, too—she has to go in and identify the Darington things. Margaret, they are absolutely gorgeous—the pearls, I mean. I've never seen anything like them in my life."

"Do you suppose they'd let us...? I didn't get to see them, darn it. Had them in my hand, too." Margaret sighed wistfully.

"It's the least they can do. You deserve all the consideration the police can give. They'd never have cracked the case without you, dear."

"And you! We did it, didn't we?"

"We certainly did."

Margaret finished her breakfast and they went upstairs to see Sybil, who declared she wouldn't dream of identifying the Darington jewels unless they were present, so that was all right. They only had to wait until five o'clock and go with her to the police station.

Back in their own room, Judy said, "What shall we do until five?"

"We could go out and see some more of the town. Is that our door?"

"No, Sybil's, next door."

The partition between their room and Sybil's was thin as cardboard and quite translucent to sound. Margaret said, "Shhh, its Inspector Lamb," and listened without shame.

"May I come in?" the Inspector asked.

"I suppose so," Sybil replied. "Thank you for calling about the jewels. I'm glad they've been recovered. And the murderer caught, too, of course. Congratulations."

"Thank you, but that's not why I came." Lamb added something else, too low to be heard.

For a few minutes there was no sound. Margaret and Judy exchanged looks—whatever was going on in there? Then they heard heavy gasps. In a voice thick with passion, Lamb blurted,

"Marry me, Sybil. I love you. I'd die for you. Please, don't push me away—I care for you. Marry me..."

"Oh, God. Go away! No! Leave me alone, you know nothing about me."

More gasps and sounds of bumped furniture. Margaret had her fist raised to pound on the wall when the door slammed and Lamb's footsteps retreated down the hall. She lowered her hand, grateful not to have to intervene. "Well! He got his come-uppance, didn't he?" She couldn't help it if that sounded vindictive; Inspector Lamb was not in her good graces.

Somehow, they got through the afternoon. They walked in Penlee Park and browsed the shops on Causeway Head. Judy bought a hot pot and had it wired for the 240 volt outlets in their room, "so we don't have to taste the kettle in our tea."

At 4:30, they came back to the hotel lobby and sat on the bench to wait for Sybil. "Poor Molly," Margaret said. "What will happen to her?"

"She was still being questioned when I left the station. They can't make her testify against her husband, can they? You can see she's terrified of Jake. Will they charge her for trying to mail the cassettes?"

"I hope not. She really didn't know anything, did she? She may have suspected, but she didn't know. He used her, that's all."

"Look; Inspector Lamb."

Lamb strode through the entrance as briskly as ever, showing no outward signs of his rejection. Still, when he saw Margaret he seemed to lose confidence. He approached gingerly and took off his hat. "Mrs. Millet, how do you feel? What did the doctor say about your head?"

"What doctor?" Margaret snapped. She wouldn't make it easy for him. "After all, I only imagined someone hit me."

Lamb had the grace to laugh. "Can you ever forgive me? I hated to be so brutal, but I had to stop you from taking any more risks."

"Well, this is a new approach."

"You see, Jake Arvin's fingerprints were on the letter—the letter addressed to you and delivered by hand on the night of the murder. When we questioned him about it, he said he'd handled the mail on the desk at the Monarch, and we couldn't prove otherwise, but we've been keeping an eye on him, all along."

Margaret looked up at him, wide eyed. "Then we didn't really solve the case?"

"Oh, yes! You did! If Mrs. Hark hadn't stopped Molly from mailing that package, we'd have no evidence. Our man was following Jake—and Jake didn't address the package to himself. It was sent to someone we had no line on. The jewels would have been lost, without you."

"Someone you had no line on? You mean you were checking his mail in the U.S.?"

"Exactly. And we're checking this new party now. Anyone who receives stolen jewels is of interest, both to us and to the American police."

"I had no idea," Margaret said.

Sybil came down the staircase on Malcolm's arm, looking radiantly lovely. Nothing like a proposal to make a girl bloom, Margaret thought, then chided herself for being snide. Of course Sybil was radiant, with her family gems recovered, the murderer caught, and her scapegrace brother cleared, at least as far as the murders were concerned.

Malcolm looked unbearably clean and wholesome in a crisp white shirt and dark red tie. His sport coat barely camouflaged his impressive shoulders. Why couldn't the girl see what was right beside her?

"Shall we go, ladies?" Malcolm asked.

"I brought a car," Lamb offered.

"Thank you, I prefer to walk." Sybil was cool as a mountain spring. And walk they did, all the way to the police station; a proud, four-person, international parade, though their banners were invisible to the world at large.

A chauffeur-driven Bentley had stopped in front of the Police Station. As they got closer, the uniformed driver jumped out and opened the rear door for his passenger; a tall fiftyish man, erect in carriage, his tailoring as impeccable as his transportation. This must be Sir Augustus Cromarth, the owner of the Cromarth collection.

The chauffeur closed the car door and dashed to open the station entrance. Sir Augustus paused on the sidewalk to inspect the approaching party. To inspect Sybil with a gracious, approving smile. In an elegant gesture of admiration, he doffed his homburg, revealing dark, neatly trimmed hair with a touch of grey at the temples. Sybil flashed her gleaming smile. Sir Augustus ushered her through the station door and followed her in, cutting Malcolm off as easily as one would discard the wrapping on a lovely present. The chauffeur's face was impassive, but Margaret caught the twinkle in his eye.

Chief Inspector Nail met them inside, and while he didn't get down on his knees, his manner was conciliatory enough to make Margaret repress a giggle. He led the way to his office where Inspector Lamb, who had got there first by car, stood guard over the jewels.

"Oh, yes," Sir Augustus said. "Let me see..." He named each gleaming gem as he took it out of the evidence box, unwrapped it, and laid it on the desk. Sybil stood at his side, ready to claim her property, but he made no errors, passing the Darington pieces to her as he found them. They reminded Margaret of children dividing their marbles; here's an aggie for you, here's my shooter, there's your cats-eye.

"We'll have to keep them in evidence for the time being," Inspector Lamb said.

Sir Augustus thought not. "I've been in touch with your superiors, young man. Call the Yard—you'll find I have authority to reclaim my property. Photographs, if you like, but the jewels go to my bank. On no account would I leave them here." He said "here" with a world of meaning; here in this insecure, provincial police station, guarded by bucolic bumblers—all that was implicit in the word.

"Miss Darington, would you care to accept my escort to London? You could take your things to safety, too. My chauffeur is also my bodyguard and he's a most capable man, my dear. You and your gems would be perfectly safe and I'd be most honored to have your company."

Sybil smiled and turned to Margaret and Judy. "Do come and look." She draped the pearls over her jade green blouse and turned her body to show them in the best light. Every man in the room held his breath. "These are for Richard's bride, someday. Won't she be lucky?" She put the diamond sunburst against her breast and said, "My great, great aunt Ophelia wore this to Victoria's coronation." Then she slipped on a magnificent ruby ring, tossed back her tawny hair, and held her hand high. "This one is mine, as the eldest daughter. It's good to see it again." She made a charming picture and her clear, musical voice cast a potent spell over them all. No one moved to break it until the last piece had been displayed.

From her heart, Margaret said, "Thank you. I'll never see anything like that again."

Displays of wealth had little power to move her or excite her envy. She had no envy now and gave no thought to the monetary value of the gems. She saw only that Sybil and the jewels belonged together. Surely such things—and such people—had their place in the world, purely for the sake of beauty.

A photographer came in and Lamb called Scotland Yard. A little later, he and Malcolm joined the ladies at the curb to say goodbye to Sybil. They watched the luxurious Bentley out of sight, and Margaret couldn't decide who looker sicker, Christopher Lamb or Malcolm Trewbridge.

Walking back to the hotel, Malcolm said, "You see, Mrs. Millet, I never had a chance with her."

"Yes, I see. I'll never understand it, but I see."

"You don't understand the English, that's all. She's out of my class. I've always known that."

Chapter 29
Mrs. Hark: Farewell to Penzance

"I don't believe she even stopped at the hotel to pick up her clothes!" Judy said, when the ladies were back in their room.

"I'm sure all her needs will be provided," Margaret replied. "Sybil has only to say, and her wishes will be granted. I do think she might have tried to get her brother out of jail before she left, though."

"Oh, she didn't forget Richard. Just before she got in the car, she took me aside and said, 'tell Richard I'll be in touch.'"

"Was that it—I wondered. And did you deliver the message?"

"I left a note with the desk sergeant. I wish we didn't have to go back there in the morning."

"I'll be glad when it's over, too," Margaret said.

"Yes. When we've told them everything and signed the statements. Then the rest of the week will be free; no more questions! Incidentally, I'm starving. I never did get any lunch."

"I wish Malcolm wouldn't go," Margaret said. "I hate to think of him driving that little MG all the way to London tonight."

Before he left, Malcolm came to write in his notebook the name of their London hotel and their flight number from Heathrow. "I have a tour starting on Sunday, but I'll be back to see you off." He hurried away as though eager to put Penzance behind him.

"The drive will do him good, I expect. I know," Judy put up her hand, "he says he knew all along Sybil wasn't for him, but he feels pretty bad, all the same."

"Yes." Margaret sighed. "I'll never understand it. Where do you want to go for dinner?"

"Fish. This is a seaport, so we should be able to find a place that has fresh fish. How about we ask Molly Arvin to go with us?"

"And the Quists? I hope they never find out I followed them to Newlyn Harbor and thought such terrible things."

Judy grinned. "If you aren't good to me, I'll tell. Do you think Molly would mind? Going out with the Quists, I mean. She may not want to."

"You want to show her she won't be shunned because of Jake, don't you. You call the Quists and put the situation to them; you're so tactful."

"Flattery will get you somewhere. I'll call the Quists if you'll call Molly."

They stood in line at the fish shop to order traditional English fish and chips. "Take away or here?" The order girl looked hot, and a greasy lock of hair straggled over her forehead, but the fish sizzling in skillets behind her smelled fresh and good.

"Here," Judy led the others to a table in the back room.

"Not much like the Monarch," Margaret said.

"No, not much like the Monarch. That will be our standard of comparison from now on, won't it?" Judy looked around the humble establishment, well patronized by locals in everyday clothes. "I just want some good, fresh fish. Hope you don't mind?"

"Oh, no," Vicky Quist said. "This is the real England, isn't it?" She turned to Victor, who smiled and nodded.

Molly said, "The real England. That was what Jake said he wanted to get with his camera." Her eyes were puffy in her lean, sallow face. She squinted against the smoke as she lit a cigarette.

"Don't talk about it unless you want to." Judy fanned away the smoke. "We all know how hard it must be."

"But do talk if it helps," Victor added. "You're among friends here."

I coached them well, Judy thought.

The food arrived; thick slabs of whitefish, lightly floured and pan fried to a golden brown, a basket of French fries and a bottle of malt vinegar on the side.

"French fries are chips here." Margaret sprinkled the vinegar on her fish. "And potato chips are called 'crisps.'"

After a couple of bites, Molly did talk, gratefully and at length, obviously feeling released from the terrible strain she had been under.

"Jake was so high that night he couldn't come down," she said.

"Which night, Molly?"

"The night Budge..." She hesitated. "I was in bed when he came back to our room in the Monarch, but I got up later to go to the bathroom and saw Budge's little satchel, right behind my slippers in the wardrobe. I think I knew then that something was terribly wrong."

Judy said, "It must have been dreadful for you, Molly."

Molly blinked and shook her head. "You've no idea. When I woke up the next morning, Jake wasn't there and neither was the satchel. I told myself I'd imagined it."

"He was at the Pettit, stuffing it in my suitcase," Judy said. "What are you going to do, Molly?"

"I don't know. I told them everything, and they said I wouldn't have to testify at the trial. I couldn't do that. If they'll let me, I'll just go home."

"We're headed for London tomorrow," Vicky said. "Maybe we can take the same train."

"Yes," Victor chimed in. "There's still time to make the Stephen Brant showing and take in the sights before we fly home."

The conversation veered to the fashion world and the delights of London. Judy looked around the fish shop with satisfaction; this had been the right atmosphere to make Molly see that the world still orbited the sun and she was not, after all, friendless and alone in a foreign land.

Thursday morning the ladies dutifully signed their statements at the Police Station, in the same back room, surrounded by the same mustard-colored walls, where they had been interrogated the day after Budge's murder.

"I don't care if I never see another police station." Judy gathered up her handbag and sweater.

They met Jake Arvin in the hallway, in handcuffs and leg chains, followed by a uniformed constable. To let him pass, Judy stepped behind Margaret who met his green-eyed glare like a snake-hypnotized sparrow.

Jake and the constable moved on and the door of the interrogation room closed behind them. Judy said, "I never saw such poison in a man's eyes. Pure hatred."

Margaret unfroze with a start and shuddered. "Let's get out of here."

As an antidote, they put on their walking shoes and hiked east and south around Mount's Bay to Marazion. The tide was coming in, so they couldn't cross the natural causeway to St. Michael's Mount; disappointing, but not important compared to the good exercise in the fresh, salty breeze from the Atlantic Ocean.

They lunched—another cream tea—in Marazion. "Here it's called Cornish Cream," Margaret said.

"I believe it's a darker yellow, too," Judy was content to rest her leg muscles and talk about food. They rode the bus back to Penzance.

During the days that followed, idle pleasure was the theme. A short flight to the Scilly Isles, a visit to the stalls of Market Jew Street on market day, walks around the town to admire and photograph such sights as the ancient brick Sailor's Rest Building and the colorful row houses of Upper High Street.

Margaret admired the row houses. "I'd like to buy one and live here for the rest of my life."

"You wouldn't want to be so far from your family," Judy said. "Be practical, Margaret."

"Let me dream. Let me dream."

The Quists and Molly were off to London on Thursday, with many protestations of gratitude and friendship and promises to keep in touch.

On Sunday, the ladies said farewell to Penzance, personified by Mrs. Canady and the sociable black cat, Poldark. The train ride to London gave them a last view of the green countryside, punctuated by villages and towns and a glimpse of the wonderful chalk horse, carved into a hillside in ancient times.

"How much did you give the waitress at the Bond?" Judy asked.

"Five pounds. I hope it was enough. She had to carry every meal up the back stairs, you know. The kitchen's on the ground floor."

"Good. So did I. Remember that woman and her little boy on the train coming down?" Mrs. Hark chuckled. "I never knew you were such an actress."

"You were pretty good yourself. It was fun to be a famous writer. Will she pester her library for my book, do you think?"

"Without a doubt."

Chapter 30
Mrs. Millet: A Penfold At Last

London was a magic city—everything Margaret Millet had dreamed it would be and more, with just enough practical discomfort to keep her from flying clear out of reality.

Gaddon Hall, one of the small hotels that line Bedford Place near the British Museum, gave them a narrow room with two single beds, a wardrobe with hooks instead of a hanger bar, a small desk with one chair, and a wash stand that burped when the faucet was turned on in the room above. The toilets and showers were down the hall, three of each in tiny cubicles. The toilets did flush on the first try, but the shower heads were seven feet high and emitted such a fine spray that it was hard to get wet, let alone rinse off the soap.

On her fifth night in the city, after an evening at the theater, Margaret sat at the desk to write to her daughter, Laura.

"If I had come all the way for this one day and then gone home again, it would have been worth it!" she wrote. "I've just seen the musical, 'Me and My Girl,' not to be confused with 'For Me and My Gal,' the American song. This show is a revival of a 1937 musical that played in London all through the Blitz. Lavishly staged and English—no, London—in the way that "West Side Story" and "Funny Girl" are New York. The plot: A Cockney lad from Lambeth falls heir to the Earldom of Hereford, but refuses to give up his Cockney sweetheart, even to attain the title.

"The couple next to us knew all the songs and sang along—they were the right age to have learned them from the original show. When the cast started 'Doing the Lambeth Walk,' the audience wouldn't let them stop, and they came down off the stage and danced in the aisles while everybody in the theater sang at the top of their lungs. Don't ever tell me the British are stolid and unfeeling. It's not true.

"We saw 'The Mousetrap,' too, in the lovely old St. Martin's Theater; mahogany paneling and railings, and just the right size for plays. I know 'The Mousetrap' by heart, of course, but it was beautifully done and after 35 years, they still ask the audience not to give away the surprise ending.

"We took one look through the British Museum and decided we wouldn't live long enough to see it thoroughly. Took lots of pictures of the wrought iron lamps and sculptures on the Embankment for Tiny. Took a boat ride to Greenwich, where the Cuttysark and the Gypsy Moth are both on display. London is no longer a real seaport. Since the tidal barrier was built, ships dock well downstream and the London stretch of the Thames is a pleasure-boat lake. Warehouses are converted to expensive flats, selling for 150,000 to 200,000 pounds (almost twice that in dollars)!

"The weather is colder, almost freezing at night. I wore a sweater under my jacket today. Judy loved Harrod's, and I wish I could bring home some of the small scale English furniture I saw at the Army and Navy Stores. Tomorrow, we have tickets for 'Cats.' I must re read T.S. Eliot's 'Book of Practical Cats' when I get home, to identify the characters.

"Then there are the parks, the palace, Big Ben, and the Peter Pan Statue, carved with animals and fairies, maybe the best of all. If the plane crashes on the way home, don't grieve for me, I'll have died happy."

And then it was over. Except for one sweater of Scottish wool, Margaret had not bought any English clothes (it was the year women's clothes, rack after rack in the stores, were all black, as though the female population of England had gone into mourning for the sorry state of the world), but she had spent all her cash. She gave her last pound coin to the maid who had, more or less, cleaned their room.

Malcolm turned up with a borrowed car to carry them and their luggage to Heathrow Airport. "Pan American Terminal? Oh, I can find it all right. I'm a bus driver then, aren't I?"

He dropped them and their luggage at the entrance and went off to park the car. The large suitcases were already checked when he reappeared to escort them and their carry-on bags through the metal detectors.

When Judy's bag emerged from the X-ray machine, a uniformed guard carried it to a table several yards distant from the passing tide of travelers.

"Here, where are you taking my bag?"

"Would you open this, please?"

"Sure. What's the matter?"

The guard looked at her searchingly. "Just open it, madam." So she did.

"A metal cylinder. Take it out, please."

"A metal cylinder! What on earth—oh, is this it?" Judy felt under her pajamas and brought out the hot pot she had bought in Penzance to make tea. It did have a tall, cylindrical shape.

Margaret and Malcolm laughed at the relief on the guard's face. "That must have looked like a bomb in the x-ray machine," Margaret said. "My friend, the dangerous terrorist."

"Don't mention that word." Malcolm took her arm. "May we go? I'll vouch for these two. They're not as dangerous as they look."

The guard laughed too, and waved them into the terminal.

The flight was delayed—a two hour wait. "Don't wait, Malcolm," Judy said. "We can't go wrong from here."

"Two hours more of your company. I'll stay, if you don't mind."

Margaret beamed. "How could we mind. Meeting you was

one of the nicest things that ever happened." Indeed, she found it hard to leave Malcolm. He had become very dear to her in the short time she had known him.

Judy looked around the terminal. "I still have some English money. Is there someplace I can exchange it?" There was, and she left them briefly, coming back with a gaudy tabloid newspaper in her hand.

"Margaret, would you look at this! And we were feeling sorry for her!"

Glaring headlines; CROMARTH COLLECTION RECOVERED, KILLER'S WIFE TELLS ALL!!!!! EXCLUSIVE TO THE DAILY BLURT, Horrifying Murders Solved, Priceless Gems Recovered, Wife Tells Story of Torture Ordeal

A three column picture of Molly Arvin topped the story. "I knew my husband was a cold-blooded murderer when he tried to use me to get rid of the loot."

There was more—lots more. Margaret and Judy were mentioned as "friends who stood by me" and Freddie Factor became a hero who tried to intervene and was tragically slain in the attempt.

"Wonder how much she got paid for this little lot," Malcolm said.

Margaret shook her head. It was past knowing. "Who would have thought Molly needed attention this badly." Her mouth felt dry. She rummaged in her purse for a vitamin C drop, and managed to spill her comb, lipstick, and a crumpled envelope. Malcolm bent to pick them up, getting down on one knee to reach the lipstick that had rolled under the bench.

"What's this, Margaret?" He turned the envelope in his hand, a look of amazement on his face.

"What? Oh, that. So many things happened, I never did get around to calling them. It's a list of the Penfolds in Cornwall. My relations, maybe, if you go back far enough."

"Penfold! But Margaret, me mum was a Penfold! This is my Aunt Maud, and Jesse is my cousin. I'm half a Penfold, too!"

And glad of it, by his huge grin. He got up off the floor and opened his arms wide.

"Malcolm! Judy—I've found my English family!" Margaret rose to be hugged and hug back with all her might.

"Hooray!" Judy cried, joining in the hugs. "You must come to California and visit us, Malcolm."

When they sat down again, Malcolm held both of Margaret's hands in a strong, enveloping clasp.

"Why, Margaret," Judy said, "What's the matter? It's just wonderful!"

Margaret lifted brimming eyes. "I don't want to go home."

It's true, she thought. I don't want to go home. Suddenly, her perfectly good, satisfactory, everyday life was ashes in her mouth. Back to cleaning and painting and repairing her rentals, pinching her pennies and saving her dimes for a rainy day. No more wonderful London shows. No more historic and beautiful places. No more walks beside the sea in Penzance. Goldy Greening, that fascinating woman, in jail. Jake Arvin in jail, green eyes and all! No more excitement. No more Sybil and Malcolm.

"I don't want it to end!" Mrs. Millet said. "No more Devonshire Cream."

An ex-chemist, teacher and bookstore owner, Margaret Searles writes (and loves) the traditional mystery. Her stories and articles have appeared in *Whispering Willow, Sleuthhound* (contest winner), *Futures MYSTERY Anthology Magazine* (Fire To Fly Award), *Mystery Readers Journal*, the SLO Death Anthologies, *New Times*, and other publications. She holds memberships in Sisters in Crime and Mystery Writers of America.

DEVONSHIRE CREAM is the second book in the Mrs. Millet & Mrs. Hark mystery series. TERLINGUA ALE, the first of the series, was published by Wrinklers Press in May, 2005.

Printed in the United States
42063LVS00002B/109